I0693965

LOADING

CAGER KLARXON

SURRENDER
POINT
PRESS

Surrender Point Press
an imprint of dFRAE Media Co.
Los Angeles, California USA

ISBN 979-8-89965-595-1 (Paperback)
ISBN 979-8-89965-656-9 (Hardcover)
ISBN 979-8-89778-754-8 (E-Book)
ISBN 979-8-89965-651-4 (Audiobook)
Library of Congress Control Number 2025905071

Edited by Ned Frazer
Book Design, Interior Art & Direction by David Sparks
Cover Illustration by @art_cofam
Dust Jacket Design by B.J. Polly
Audiobook Narration by Troy SF

This edition is typeset in Spectral, designed by Jean-Baptiste Levée for Production Type. Licensed under the SIL Open Font License, Version 1.1.

The characters and events in this book are fictitious. Any resemblance to real persons, living or dead, is purely coincidental and not intended by the author.

First printing October 2025
Second printing, revised, July 2026

Visit

www.cagerklarxon.com

www.surrenderpointpress.com

LOADING...

This book is for all of my brothers from other mothers.

Contents

B EFORE WE BEGIN, THE algorithm requires the following disclosure:

This content has been flagged for gore, male pregnancy, reproductive horror, forced modification, parasitic infection, torture, blood, vomiting, explicit sexual content, sex work, BDSM, impact play, taboo sexual dynamics, cult activity, group manipulation, childhood trauma, dissociation, drugging, extreme online harassment, and doxing.

By reading past this, you can't say you didn't know.

Listen, this isn't a story you'll wanna tell at parties.

This is what crawls out when the screen gets a hard-on for your eyeballs. When the line between you and the filth blurs into a sticky mess.

You came for cheap thrills? You'll leave colonized.

What follows is raw. Explicit. A mirror reflecting our sick hunger for content. It's a necessary infection. A portrait of a world where nothing's too extreme, too private, or too sacred to be sold.

This ain't gonna hold your hand or give you a happy ending. It will crawl under your skin and violate your safe space. Just like our screens have dissolved what's public and what's private. What's human and what's machine?

There are no safe words here. So buckle the fuck up. You've been warned.

So...

Here we go.

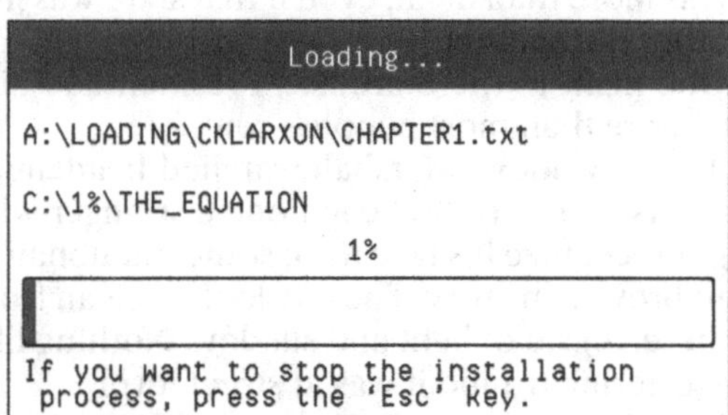

DESIRE IS A COLD, hard math. Marshall knew the equation like he knew the price of a Thread City fuck. Thirty-two years old, and his body was a finely tuned engine, purring for the right touch, the right heat.

Back when he was Markus Jensen, a marketing student with a head for numbers and a face that made his professors drool, he'd been a different program. That life crashed and burned ten years and a name change ago, when his college advisor, Ellie Webb, caught him shooting amateur porn in his dorm. Her offer was simple: expulsion or withdrawal.

"Whatever you're chasing," she'd said, her eyes dead with disappointment as they scanned the camera setup, "I hope you find it before it *fucks* you up."

Her words still echoed. He *knew* what he was chasing: the hungry stare of someone who saw him as more than meat, even if that stare was just another transaction.

One night in the Stardust's Presidential Suite cost more than most people's rent.

At the window, Marshall watched headlamps crawl like veins of fire, each one a stranger who might recognize his face from some thumbnail in their browser history. The city looked clean from up here. A grid of light and shadow. Nothing like the festering wound it was at street level.

His phone vibrated on the marble counter-top, spitting out the usual digital cum: medical alerts, subscription renewals, booking confirma-tions, fan messages edging into thirst as the night deepened. Each one was a promise or a threat. He'd stopped telling them apart.

Kate's name flashed up, his kid sister. The only blood tie that hadn't snapped. *Markus's* sister, really. Marshall barely knew her. Her text was short:

[Text Message - Kate]

Dad's in hospice. Been asking for you. Real name, not your work name. Call me?

Marshall stared at the screen, his fingers twitching over the keypad. *Markus. He wants Markus.* The name was a ghost from a discarded operating system.

Their father the math professor, a mind of elegant proofs and inescapable conclusions. He had executed his own social calculation when the first videos leaked.

"No son of mine sells his dignity!" he'd choked out, his voice cracking with a rage that hid behind a thin veneer of intellect.

Eight years of silence. Now he was dying, a countdown to zero. A hot, unwelcome pressure built behind his eyes. He refused to name it. He shoved it down, smothered it under cold professionalism.

What would closure look like on camera? he thought. The cynicism was a familiar shield. *The ultimate confessional content?*

He swiped the notification away. A subroutine to terminate. Family could wait. The algorithm of Marshall didn't allow for personal glitches.

The city lights painted his skin in neon-blue from a distant sign licking his shoulder, red from a traffic light staining his throat.

They think it's about the sex, he thought. *They're fucking wrong. It's about the emptiness. It's about holes that need filling.*

Marshall hadn't always been this hollow. Each follower gained, each subscriber added, each viral moment was another scoop scraping away the flesh of who he'd been. His personality, his dreams, his fucking connections—hollowed out and replaced by metrics, engagement stats, the cold calculus of what performed. What remained was a shell with a fixed, glowing grin for the crowd.

His first real video was for Jake, his college boyfriend with the soft hands and film school fantasies. "Just for us," Jake had promised. Six months later, after their messy breakup, those private moments were splattered across three different platforms. Jake's revenge, a pathetic grab for fame, had launched Marshall's career. Within weeks, the video blew up and offers poured in. His advisor's disgust and his father's rejection just sharpened his focus. If intimacy was a knife in the back, then transaction was a condom: Protection. Distance. Control.

His follower count hit seven digits last month. Seven digits of hungry eyes, fingers, and fantasies, all glued to his masterful performance. Of these, maybe fifteen people knew his real name. Three knew where he grew up. None knew why the smell of Pine-Sol made him want to puke or why he hoarded hotel soaps in a box under his bed.

The scent memory flashed. Hiding in a closet at six years old, his stepfather's rage a chainsaw in their trailer. The pine cleaner his mother used to scrub away the evidence afterward.

DELETE.

Marshall shoved the memory back into its cage. *No room for that shit now. Focus on the variables at hand.*

[Calendar Notification]

PRIVATE SESSION - Presidential Suite 1414. Group of 12 - Special Requests Noted. Deposit Received: $7,500. Remainder Due: Cash on Arrival

His agent, Victor, called as Marshall began his prep. *Predictable.* He dumped the call to voicemail, the ringtone a jarring interruption to his ritual. Victor had been his pit bull for seven years. Less a friend, more a necessary functionary in the business of Marshall. He'd pulled Marshall from the amateur gutter, negotiated his first deals, pushed him to the high-roller market when others wanted to pimp his youth for quick cash. His commission was a bitch, a significant percentage skimmed, but his protection was usually solid.

Tonight's booking, however, had slipped through the back door. A direct wire, bypassing Victor's usual meticulous, almost paranoid vetting. He'd shit a brick if he knew. Or maybe he already suspected.

The voicemail notification blinked. Marshall let it wait until he was toweling off, the steam clinging to the bathroom.

[Voicemail - Victor]

▶ /// *Marshall, I just got wind of this Stardust booking. Twelve clients? No fucking background checks? This ain't you. This isn't US. Call me NOW. Whatever they're paying, it ain't worth the risk. We've built too much to gamble on unknowns.*

He was right, of course. Victor's risk assessment was usually spot on. But Kate's text message burned in his mind, a connection to a life he'd tried to amputate. He hadn't spoken to his father in eight fucking years, and now a deathbed summons for *Markus*. The name felt like a genital wart that kept coming back, no matter how much acid was put on it.

The money was in record territory. That wasn't the point. This booking was an act of defiance. A way to burn away the last remnants of the boy his father was asking for. For Marshall, the risk *was* the profit, and tonight's profit was oblivion.

Hotel rooms, temporary flesh. For hours or days, they belong to whomever pays the tab. They hold no memory, no judgment. Only the top-shelf suites met Marshall's needs: sound-proofing, multiple exits, staff who knew the value of looking the fuck away.

The Stardust's Presidential Suite was perfect. Big enough for a crowd, tight enough to capture everything on camera. The lighting could be tweaked to flatter. The bathroom had open showers and a tub big enough for a fucking orgy. The sheets were Egyptian cotton.

Marshall's ritual: enema, then shower. Face cream, then body oil. Phone check, equipment check. Cash verification. Hush money for the hotel staff, already paid.

Another vibration. Kate again. This time, a call. He glanced. Sent it to voicemail and continued his grooming ritual.

Five minutes later, Kate's name flashed up again. This time, a text.

[Text Message - Kate]

Markus, I know you're working but he's got days at most…

Days. Just a unit of time. He had a performance to prepare for. Twelve variables. Unknown factors. High stakes.

This was what mattered tonight. The math of Marshall. The hustle. It was a balancing act.

Too many sessions cheapened the product. Too few starved the bank account, risked fading into obscurity. Each encounter had to be exclusive enough to bleed them dry, yet frequent enough to stay relevant in the attention-whore economy. His body was the product, the marketing, and the means of production. Late-stage capitalism at its most fucked, and he was a master of it.

He set up a camera on a tripod near the bed. Two smaller, more discreet others would grab different angles. The illusion of intimacy in a transaction designed to annihilate it. Raw footage would be edited later, packaged into digestible content ready for the masses. Another offering to the insatiable digital maw.

His success grew straight out of his hollowness. He cultivated it like others cultivate a goddamn garden, pruning away any inconvenient shoots of genuine emotion. It made him a better performer. A blanker canvas for their projections.

He reached into his bag and pulled out a small, worn teddy bear. Placed it on the bedside table, just in frame. An odd variable. It was his grandma's last gift, the only person who'd ever looked at Marshall—at *Markus*—and seen HIM. Not what he could give, not a body to be used or a problem to be solved. Sometimes during system reboots, between gigs, he'd clutch it and try to remember what it felt like. Unconditional. The word felt foreign.

His grandma had raised him for three years during his mother's first rehab stint. When he was eight, she'd read to him every night, her soft voice painting worlds beyond their shitty, cramped apartment. *"You have a light in you,"* she'd whisper, stroking his hair. *"Don't let anyone dim it."*

A bitter laugh almost escaped. *Dim it? Grandma, I turned it into a fucking ring light for close-ups.*

After her funeral, his spiraling mother had packed them up and moved in with Terry. The stepfather whose rage would force Marshall into closets, clutching this same bear to muffle his sobs. The Pine-Sol a nauseating miasma of fear and erased evidence. He wondered what she would think of him now. Of the light he'd twisted into a spotlight for his performance. Of how it burned bright but illuminated nothing. Just the contours of manufactured lust.

His phone vibrated again. Victor, calling for the third time. The persistence was irritating. A buzzing fly in the otherwise controlled environment of the suite. Marshall silenced it without looking. Victor's warnings, his anxieties, were his own problem.

[Text Message - Number Redacted]

we're downstairs. 12 of us. special request still good?

Marshall hesitated, his thumb hovering over reply. The shadowy go-between who made the booking mentioned "authenticity," "pushing limits," "fantasies that required specific, unmediated conditions." The extra cash had been enough to override Victor's protocols. To drown his better judgment. It was a risk, another complex variable in his ongoing experiment.

[Text Message - Marshall]

> Suite 1414. Special request confirmed. No faces in footage as agreed.

After sending the text, Marshall killed his phone, severing the connection to the outside world. Victor's hand-wringing could wait until morning. Until after the transaction was complete. He adjusted the cameras one last time, checking the frames, ensuring the supporting cast would remain anonymous blurs. Their identities were irrelevant. The room was set. The stage prepped. Marshall's body was the main event.

In the seconds before they arrived, alone in the silence of the suite, an unbidden Jake memory surfaced. He'd polished that narrative into a clean, convenient lie for years. What had really twisted the knife back then was the power play. Jake's attempt to control *his* narrative, to define *him* without his fucking say-so.

Part of him, the part that was already becoming Marshall, had been relieved. Jake's betrayal was the perfect excuse. A trigger to pull on an already loaded weapon. Deep down, Markus Jensen had always been this hungry. This desperate to be seen. Marshall had simply seized the opportunity to fire.

Now Jake shot wedding videos in some dead-end town, his film school dreams reduced to capturing strangers' happiness. Marshall's net worth had crawled into seven figures. The market had spoken.

The thought dissolved as three sharp knocks echoed through the suite. Showtime.

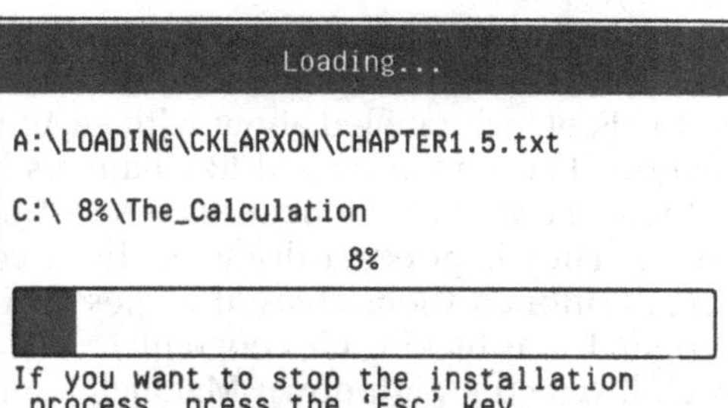

THE FIRST MAN THROUGH the door was a wall of muscle, hands that looked like they could strangle Marshall's throat completely. Not the usual type. The others followed, a silent procession. Twelve men in total, ranging from late twenties to mid-fifties. They were dressed in clothes that said money but didn't flash it.

Their eyes, though, shared a common hunger. A wolfish gleam leashed beneath the layer of expensive manners. Marshall cataloged them, running quick threat assessments. His internal processor flagged multiple anomalies.

"The famous Marshall," the tall one said. His baritone voice carried across the suite. His eyes were scanning, dissecting. A slow rape of Marshall's body, yes, but colder. More analytical than the usual slobbering appraisal. "Even better in the flesh."

Flesh. Just meat.

They shed their coats and spread through the suite. Marshall noticed something else. He was used to clients who milled about with eager anticipation. These men moved like dancers hitting their marks, or a tactical team securing a location. They kept exact distances from each other. Positioned themselves at angles around the room. It was fucking choreography.

A chill traced a path down Marshall's spine. His internal threat level ticked up a notch.

The tall one stepped forward. Posture tight. His eyes were clear blue and sharp as scalpels. They sliced into Marshall's face, devoid of the usual cloudy thirst that made men easy to manipulate. This was different.

This was... unsettling.

"Name's Daniel," he said. A tiny smile touched his lips. "Not that names matter much, do they? What matters is you get it. This wasn't random, Marshall."

Marshall's throat constricted. *Not random?* His fingers made an aborted twitch. The phone was across the room. His lifeline to Victor, to the script of the world. A self-imposed isolation for 'focus'.

"They saw you," Daniel continued, a slight nod to the other eleven men. They were like wax figures, eyes latched onto Marshall with a flat, collective stare. Zero affect. "The perfect fit. Someone already... clearing out the space, you could say. Long before we showed up."

Marshall swallowed. His mouth tasted like pennies. *Fit? Space?* The words felt sterile.

Wrong. He struggled to keep his professional veneer from cracking. The hollow shell he'd offered the world suddenly felt like a self-fulfilling prophecy. This was twisted. But... he tried to remind himself that the twisted often had the deepest pockets. He just needed the angle.

"I'm not following the '*fit*' part," he said, his voice surprisingly even. Years of practice. "But look, whatever fantasy you're here to play out, I'm your guy. That's what the money's for, right?" His attempt at smiling made his lips feel like they were pulling back from his teeth.

One of the others stepped forward. Forty-something, wire-frames. The disdain of a tenured radical. He drifted closer. "We've observed your... performances... for some time, Marshall," he said. His voice was quiet. "Not for the usual reasons, I assure you. We detected a certain... methodology. A detachment. We can see you've been, shall we say, curating your own emptiness." He pushed his glasses up his nose, his eyes unwavering. Dissecting. "Most people fight to hold onto who they are. You seem to be dismantling it."

Observed? Methodology? This was way outside. His internal schematics were failing, the data refusing every known category.

"We need to start," said a younger man. A neatly sculpted beard. A rapid mechanical tic in his left eyelid. "The window is... precise."

Daniel gave a definitive nod. "No need for the usual song and dance tonight, Marshall. You know why we're here." His eyes passed over Marshall's groin, the customary target. They fixed on his navel, an unnerving focal point. "To fill that space you've made!"

Then, as if summoned by Daniel's words, the money materialized. Pristine, banded stacks of hundreds on the table. Warmth spread through Marshall's chest, the current that always hummed low in his gut at this part. This was the anchor. Whatever unsettling script these men were following, crisp cash was a language Marshall understood. His favorite moment, honestly. The tangible proof of his magnetism in the room.

One of the silent figures moved to count it, fingers flicking through the bills. Marshall watched, a true smile playing on his lips. *Let them be mechanical. The transaction was underway.*

The cash vanished into the room safe. The click of the tumblers. A satisfying, decisive sound. It sealed their pact. Only then did the cold edge of the situation creep back in.

"Ground rules," Marshall said, pushing back. Trying to reclaim some semblance of control, to steer this back towards recognizable territory. "Safe words—'Red Stop,' 'Yellow Slow.' Expectations are clear. The cameras are rolling, boundaries will be respected. This is a transaction with clear limits, a performance with willing players." He needed them to acknowledge the framework, his framework.

Daniel smiled. A shark's smile. All teeth, no warmth. It promised nothing but a clean, efficient kill. "Of course, Marshall. We respect your... professional standards." The slight emphasis on 'professional' was a subtle mockery. "This is a transaction, as you say. Though perhaps not quite the one you're expecting."

What followed was the formula Marshall thought he knew by heart. The choreography of commercial passion. But it twisted into new territory, throwing his internal gyroscope off balance. The famous porn star, Marshall, had been in his share of gangbangs. Multi-partner scenes that pushed boundaries, but always within a framework he controlled or could navigate. Nothing, however, could prepare him for this.

The room, already charged, now reeked of testosterone and an undercurrent he couldn't name. The air thick with the promise of something brutal.

As the men stripped, Marshall's eyes widened. His professional composure faltered. These weren't the usual gym-bunny fuckboys or fellow content creators looking for a collab. These were real men. Their bodies varied. Some hard and muscled, others softer, older, but all exuding a raw, primal hunger. They looked like they could break him. To his horror, and to some buried, shameful part of him, the thought was a little bit hot. A dangerous new variable.

His body became their stage. The math was still there, in a way. Each man would get his turn. Each angle would be captured for the unseen audience. Each moment designed to maximize the money shot.

The "special request," the one that came with the massive bonus, was another variable. A substance they brought themselves, presented now by Daniel in a small, clear glass vial with a dropper. Amber liquid swirled inside.

"It just enhances things," Daniel explained. His proximity was absolute. His eyes, those sharp blue scalpels, were terrifying. "Makes you mor e... receptive."

Marshall's throat seized. The professional facade he'd worn for years finally, visibly, fractured. The amber liquid in the small vial Daniel held seemed to throb with a dim, internal light. A captured, restless energy. Alarms shrieked through his mind. *Receptive to what?*

"What is it?" he asked. The question felt like a tiny, pathetic shard of defiance. A grab for a control that had already bled out. His voice was barely audible even to himself.

Daniel moved even closer, the vial now extended like an offering in some unholy rite. Those piercing blue eyes never left Marshall's. "Does it really matter what it is, Marshall?" His voice was a whisper, meant for Marshall alone despite the eleven others lining the room. "You've spent years hollowing yourself out. Performance by performance, transaction by transaction. We're just offering... fullness."

Fullness. The word slammed into him, a physical blow to the void he'd cultivated. A vile seduction, whispered straight into the emptiness he pacified with attention and cash.

Marshall's eyes flicked to his phone, still dead on the nightstand. Kate's messages. His dying father, reaching out for *Markus*—the boy he'd been before the void had started to swallow him, before Marshall had engineered his own erasure. His grandma's voice, a faint, cherished echo: *"You have a light in you... Don't let anyone dim it."*

How much of that light had he already snuffed out, traded away piece by piece, even before these men, these architects of some unknown design, had arrived?

He even thought of Jake again, the villain he'd cast to justify his own descent into transactional intimacy. The catalyst for something already broken within Markus?

"I don't do drugs," Marshall said, the lie so reflexive, so automatic, it was almost convincing. The scheduled delivery of pharmaceuticals that kept his body performing. The occasional party favors indulged with high-paying clients. The morning-after pills that ensured he could keep fucking without consequence... the hypocrisy was a fucking joke, and suddenly he wasn't sure who the punchline was.

The professor—the older one, with the wire-rimmed glasses that now reminded Marshall of his own father—stepped forward. His posture was academic, his voice calm. Reasonable, which somehow made it more menacing.

"It's not a drug, Marshall. Not as you understand the term." He adjusted his glasses, the gesture almost paternal. "It's a catalyst. A key. Designed to unlock what's already there, what you've already cultivated."

His hand reached out, hovering over Marshall's shoulder, a phantom touch that sent a shiver down his spine. "You've spent your life being watched, Marshall. Performing. This is your chance to become something worth *witnessing*."

The words, damn them, resonated in a place Marshall thought long dead, a place starved of genuine significance. The eternal human hunger—not just to be seen, but to be *seen as important*. To matter. To be more than disposable content in an endless, scrolling feed. More than meat.

He stared at the vial, the amber liquid within it. *What would it feel like to be full again?* To have his core filled with something more than the fleeting high of strangers' attention?

His hand rose, trembling. A lifetime of calculated risks, of pushing boundaries while maintaining the illusion of control. This was just another performance, wasn't it? Another line crossed for the right price, the ultimate special request. The fee attached to this 'enhancement' had been enough to shut down his rational mind, to let his fear and his pragmatism reach a fucked-up, silent compromise.

Yet something deeper protested. A ghost of Markus, perhaps? Or just animal self-preservation, screaming that there would be no coming back from this?

The eleven others watched with unnerving intensity. Their breathing seemingly synchronized, expectant. Daniel's eyes, those cold pools, never left Marshall's face.

Marshall's last clear thought was that this hesitation, this final flicker of resistance, might be the most real, most *Markus* thing he'd done in years. Then his lips parted, and he took the dropper from Daniel's steady hand.

The liquid burned cold on Marshall's tongue. Sweet at first. Then bitter as bile. As it slid down his throat, he felt a line snap, a decision made that couldn't be undone. The room's familiar angles shifted, went alien, as if he were seeing the world with a layer of reality stripped away.

Marshall didn't know it yet, but the garden he'd just left could never be entered again. The equation had been solved, and he was the unknown variable, finally defined.

Daniel's hand was on his shoulder now, steadying him. "Let it happen, Marshall," he said, his voice low against the sudden roaring in Marshall's ears. "The first moments are always... disorienting."

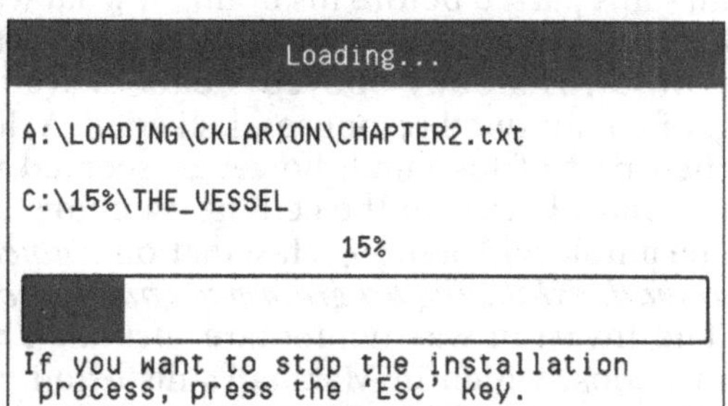

DISORIENTING WAS A FUCKING understatement.

The first man, the wall of muscle from the doorway, moved closer. Marshall felt the amber liquid spreading through his system like a digital virus. It started as a tingling in his teeth. A low hum like a faulty fluorescent light buzzing behind his eyeballs. A cold, metallic taste flooded his mouth as every nerve ending fired at once. Like licking a battery.

The room seemed to warp and breathe. Expensive, tasteful luxury furnishings twisted into grotesque, leering shapes in his peripheral vision. The tall man loomed, his body large. A caricature of masculine aggression that was terrifying and... arousing.

"Open!" the man commanded, his voice distorted, echoing like the bottom of a well. Marshall's lips parted before his brain, or what was left of its executive function, could process the order. His body obeyed. Years of training, of conditioned responses, kicked in. A detached part of his mind, however, seemed to float somewhere near the ceiling, watching the scene unfold with a strange fascination. *Subject Marshall, exhibiting programmed compliance.*

The invasion was immediate. Brutal. The man's cock, which in Marshall's distorted vision seemed as thick as his own forearm, forced its way into his mouth. From his strange, floating perspective, Marshall watched himself perform. Saw his own eyes water from the pressure. Felt the burn and the stretch of his jaw. But mixed with the familiar discomfort was a disturbing, alien pulse of pleasure. A feedback loop from some other source. The liquid twisted everything, making sensations sharper, more vivid, yet dreamlike. Reality itself became a questionable, flickering projection.

"He's responsive." The voice sounded miles away, filtered through layers of cotton. "More than the others." *Others? What others?*

A hand, not Daniel's, tightened in his hair, yanking Marshall's consciousness back into his body. Anchoring him in raw sensation. His throat opened. Years of practice, of honing this specific skill, allowed him to take the intrusion. He avoided the gag reflex that amateurs always succumbed to. A flicker of perverse pride cut through the haze. This was his skill, his brand. Even as this felt profoundly wrong, there was a professional's grim satisfaction in a job well done.

Then hands from behind. He couldn't see whose, couldn't turn. They penetrated him. One lubricated finger, then two, then three, stretching him. The room spun.

"He's perfect," a voice said—was it the professor? Daniel? The voices were blending, layering, losing their distinctiveness, becoming a single, monstrous chorus. "Look how he yields. How he stays present even as he dissociates. The ideal vessel."

Vessel. There's that word again. Marshall tried to focus, to claw back some measure of control, but the amber liquid had dissolved some crucial linkage between his will and his flesh. He'd faked surrender a thousand times, performed submission with an artist's precision. But this... this was real. His calculated resistance, his boundaries, were melting away like sugar in water. He was a passenger in his own body, watching it respond with an eagerness that horrified the fading observer in his skull.

They arranged themselves around him then, the twelve of them, forming a perfect fucking circle. A ritual formation. Marshall, at the center of their geometry, felt a jolt of pure, animal terror as he saw their cocks, each one erect, pulsing with an unnatural, inner rhythm. His fear twisted sickeningly into a desperate hunger, a need he didn't recognize. Something in him had woken up demanding to be filled.

"Please," he heard himself beg, voice raw and broken. It sounded like his porn persona, but infused with something utterly debased. "Fill me!"

The men exchanged satisfied, knowing looks, as if he'd spoken a password that granted them access to his depths. Then they descended, and Marshall's reality shattered into a million screaming fragments.

Time became meaningless. His body was a collection of holes to be violated, of nerve endings to be overloaded. They stretched him beyond what felt like human limits. Rammed down his throat, choking off his attempts to breathe, to scream. Impersonal and strong hands held him down, rearranging him like a piece of furniture. They positioned him for optimal access. For maximum exposure. Pain bloomed into pleasure and back again. The boundaries between sensation and outright violation dissolved.

Their eyes reflected the dim light of the suite at impossible angles. Their cocks, when he could bear to look, pulsed with light, as if they were animated by a force beyond biology. Then they were just twelve johns. Their faces flushed, using the meat he sold. And then they were something *other*. Silent priests performing a dark ritual with his desecrated flesh as the altar.

"He's opening," one of them said. Marshall didn't know if they meant his body, which was undeniably breached, or something deeper.

His consciousness fractured. Part of him still floated near the ceiling, a witness watching his body being used. Part of him was trapped in every stretched muscle, every fucking breach of his physical integrity. And in a shrinking corner of his mind untouched by the drug or the men, the last echo of Markus whispered that this wasn't just a gangbang. Wasn't just rough sex.

Wasn't just another transaction pushed to the extreme.

It's a conception.

Yet, even as this horrifying understanding tried to surface through the layers of sensation and surrender, Marshall found his body responding with increasing abandon. He remained hard despite the abuse. His body arched into touches that should have repulsed him, that *did* repulse the part of him that was still him. The dichotomy was excruciating. His mind, what was left of it, screamed *NO, STOP, this is wrong!* while his flesh, hijacked and rewired, begged for more.

"He's fighting it," someone observed, as Marshall's eyes rolled back. His mind was trying to claw its way back to the controls even as his body surrendered like a puppet whose strings were in their hands.

"Not for long," Daniel answered. He placed a hand on Marshall's abdomen, just below his navel. The touch burned, an intensity that made Marshall's back arch off the bed, a cry tearing from his throat that sounded nothing like his usual porn-star moans. Nothing human at all.

They used him for what felt like hours. Each combination of fucks and brutal intimacies served some hidden purpose Marshall couldn't grasp through the fog. His body was passed between them like a joint at a party, each man taking his fill before offering him to the next. Marshall felt both more hideously alive in his skin and completely divorced from it. A passenger in a body responding to their collective will.

And beneath it, terrible, undeniable pleasure. A sense that he was finally being *seen*, truly *used* for his perfect purpose. That all his years of performance had been a deliberate preparation for this single moment of absolute consumption.

"More," he begged again, the word an incoherent gasp. He didn't know what he was asking for, what more they could take or give, but he needed it with a primal desperation. "Please. More."

Daniel smiled down at him. "Yes," he said, promising oblivion. "It's time."

Marshall didn't know what "it" was, what final horror "time" had come for, but his body shuddered with a sickening anticipation that felt like a perverse kind of victory. Whatever was happening, whatever they were doing to him, a newly awakened part of him *wanted* it.

Daniel approached, holding something that gleamed in the dim light. It was small. Metallic. Precise. Surgical? Marshall felt something that hadn't been there before the amber liquid, before the twelve men, before this twisted ritual disguised as a high-end transaction, stir in recognition. A presence not his own.

"The final act," Daniel said softly. "The completion."

Marshall spread his legs wider, tilted his head back, and offered his ravaged body with a sick, eager passivity. And it felt... right. In the most wrong way imaginable. Whatever was happening, his body already craved it with an intensity that drowned out the defeated protests of his conscious mind.

"Yes," Marshall whispered, strange and resonant in his own ears. "Complete me!"

What followed transcended the fucking ordinary. Transcended even the extremities he had just endured. The object touched his abdomen, just below his navel, where Daniel's hand had burned him earlier. Pressure without pain, at first. An opening without tearing.

His consciousness, or what he thought of as his consciousness, ascended. A mist of gold. Below, his body was no longer his, but a map being rewritten. Twelve silhouettes stood in perfect formation around the bed. Silent witnesses to a perverse, unspeakable miracle. "The vessel is ready." A voice. Or a thought implanted into his shattering mind. Twelve voices becoming one voice becoming pure, disembodied code.

Marshall shattered. Perception exploded like light through a goddamn prism, refracted into a thousand parallel hells. A million digital streams. In one: the Presidential Suite. The transaction concluded. Money in the safe. Bodies spent. In another: his form dissolving into digital rain. Pixels fucking his bloodstream. Rewriting his DNA with every agonizing pulse. An invisible seam beneath his navel: no longer skin, but a port. A chalice. A gateway. A fucking genesis point. Something entering. Cum? Piss? Drugs? No, not even the amber liquid. Pure. Fucking. Information. Flooding his guts. Code raping his flesh raw from the inside out.

His veins, he could see them, *feel* them, glowing from within,
    blue lightning beneath translucent, alien skin.
    Tongues of data,
           silent
           and screaming,
replacing his own choked cries.
His cock, still
           hard,
           throbbed with an electric,

`   impossible seed.
Twelve disciples
`   of the digital, apostles of the algorithm,
`   their faces blurred, indistinct.
The walls
`   of the suite morphing into shimmering
circuit boards,
`   intricate and infinite.
The ceiling dissolving into a map of the fucking stars,
cold
`   and distant
`   and terrifyingly near.
Marshall watched, from somewhere outside
and everywhere inside, as his essence,
`   his self,
`   was compressed—
sanctified
`   in binary,
sorted,
`   indexed,
`   baptized in silicon.
His source code,
`   the very blueprint
`   of Markus Jensen and Marshall, unrav-
eling,
`   rewriting itself at an impossible speed.
Pine cleaner memory—
`   *backspace,*
`   *backspace,*
corrupting file.
Father's equations,
`   his disappointment,
`   his rejection—   *delete,*
`   *delete,*
`   *DELETE.*

Grandmother's lullaby,
      her soft touch,
         her belief in his light—
his last testament—
      AUDIO CORRUPTED.
      FILE NOT FOUND.
The device,
    the interface
        at his center: connection point estab-
lished.
ERROR: *The vessel is currently in use. Stand by*
    for full integration.
Body:
    temple
      turned meat-machine.
Mind:
    a whore
      to a higher, colder power.
His thoughts, no longer his own, scrolling like
a command prompt:
WARNING: Formatting will erase ALL data.
      To format this vessel, click OK.
      To abort, click CANCEL.
His humanity, a tiny, flickering cursor, hov-
ered
    over OK...
"It is finished!"
    they spoke-not-spoke, the words—
      if they were words— hovering,
    luminous,
    untethered from any fucking voice, from
any mouth.
System
    incarnating—

```
                        Loading...

A:\LOADING\CKLARXON\CHAPTER3.txt

C:\23%\DISINTEGRATION
                          23%

If you want to stop the installation
process, press the 'Esc' key.
```

MARSHALL JOLTED AWAKE. HIS consciousness slammed back into his body with the force of a car crash, leaving him shaking and disoriented. The Stardust's Presidential Suite reassembled itself around him in jagged, unreliable pieces. Expensive furniture askew. Rumpled, stained sheets. Abandoned camera equipment looking like sleeping, metallic insects.

The digital clock on the bedside table glowed: 3:17 AM. The men had arrived at midnight. Three hours ripped from his memory, swallowed by whatever had just happened. Or hadn't happened. Maybe it was just the drugs.

He pushed himself out of bed, his legs trembling so violently he almost collapsed. The room tilted. If they'd given him anything at all. If there had really been twelve men. If any of it was real beyond the ache between his thighs and a soreness in his abdomen. His mind groped for something solid, but found only fragments: hands, voices, the gleam of a device that might have been surgical.

The feeling of being... rewritten.

In the bathroom mirror, his reflection stared back. Marshall, looking rough around the edges, but intact. No glowing veins. He examined his body, his fingers tracing the skin where he remembered an opening, an insertion. No mark. Just a faint sense of movement inside him, so subtle it could be his pulse, his mind already conjuring proof of its most paranoid fears.

His phone screen lit up with seventeen missed calls when he finally powered it back on. Fourteen from Victor, three from Kate. Kate had sent voice notes.

[Voice Notes – Kate]

▶ /// *Listen... Dad... Dad keeps asking for you. Like, constantly, it's "Markus? Where's Markus?" His voice is... God, it's so weak. I'm sitting here, and it's... it's really hard. I know things with Dad were always... a mess. So much crap happened, so much hurt. I'm not pretending that wasn't real. But, Markus, you have to believe me... he regrets it. So much. I can see it in his eyes, what's left of them. It's like all the fight's gone out of him, and all that's left is this... this hollow regret. He's not the man he was, not anymore.*

▶ /// *I'm so worried about you. Seriously. I, um, I see your posts sometimes. Not the... you know, the other stuff, just the... the lifestyle ones. And I know you think you're hiding it well, with all the filters and the perfect captions and that smile... that smile you practice. But I know you, Markus. We grew up together, remember? Hiding how messed up we felt was practically our childhood sport. I can see when you're struggling. I just... I can tell. That look in your eyes, even when you're trying so hard... it's the same look you had when you were ten and trying to pretend everything was okay.*

▶ /// There's... there's something else too. Something I need to talk about in real time, Markus. Something weird... Call me, please!

He stared at the screen and felt... nothing. A flatline. He ignored the rest, dropping the phone back onto the marble.

Back in the desecrated bed, he fell into a dreamless sleep. An oblivion that lasted until harsh sunlight sliced through a gap in the curtains and dragged him back to consciousness. Time to check out. The city outside was grinding on. Oblivious to the horror show that had played out in Suite 1414.

In the days that followed, Marshall's body kept its secrets, or tried to. He posted content like nothing had changed. Same angles. Same lighting. Same curated moans and expressions of ecstasy. His feed stuck to its schedule: workout videos on Mondays, teaser clips on Wednesdays, premium drops on Fridays. The algorithm demanded consistency above all else. It was the god he served. Business as usual. But the comments, those tiny windows into the collective consciousness of his followers, started to show changes in perception he couldn't control:

[OnlyFans Comments]

> Marshall's, there's a new intensity in your eyes. Like you're seeing something we're not. Haunting, but a little unsettling.

> timestamp 5:32 did the focus pull weirdly at his abdomen, or was it an editing choice? Made me rewind.

Marshall deleted these comments, blocking the accounts that dared to post them. The math of social media demanded absolute control. Any hint of physical change, any deviation from the established brand, had to be his to define. To monetize and twist into new content. Not theirs to discover.

The shrill insistence of his phone finally clawed through whatever passed for sleep these days. 3 AM. Five days since... that. He'd let Victor's calls pile up. But this time, the preview of Victor's text that flashed on screen—PICK UP OR I'M COMING OVER—Marshall recognized as a promise not a threat. He swiped to answer.

"Took you long enough," Victor's voice crackled. Fury, yes, but something else too. Exhaustion. "You can't keep fucking ignoring me, Marshall. Your metrics are all over the place. Engagement's through the roof, but subscriber retention? Down 12%. Twelve percent, Marshall. What the fuck did you do in that hotel room? The footage you sent... it's like something chewed on the damn data itself."

Marshall shifted on his couch, the movement pulling at the tightness in his body. The sensation had become a hum beneath the surface of his days. "Technical glitch," he said. "I'm working on it." Working on it? He hadn't dared look at the source files again after the first attempt.

The vertical line above his groin was invisible to the eye but tangible to him. Sometimes, late at night, he could feel it pulsing. A rhythm that echoed his own heartbeat. His bathroom scale, when he'd dared to look that morning, still showed the same numbers, but his skin felt different. Stretched.

"This isn't you," Victor snarled. "You're meticulous. A control freak. Who were these clients? You ghosted the entire protocol."

Who were these clients? A name surfaced, unbidden. Not memory, more like... an imprint. "It came through an intermediary," Marshall said. "Name was Aaron Klass."

"Klass?" Victor's incredulity was palpable. "Never heard of him. And you just... took the booking? After everything we've built? Jesus, Marshall, this isn't just about chasing the fattest paycheck. There are fucking risks. Real ones."

The line below Marshall's navel gave a pulse. An acknowledgment. Or a warning.

"I'm fine," Marshall lied again. "It was just another fucking gig." But there was a tremor in his voice. He knew it was anything but.

Victor changed tactics, his voice dropping. "Your sister called me yesterday," he said. "She says you're not answering her messages about your father."

A spike of rage lanced through Marshall. Kate! Dragging his business into family shit. The line he'd fought to maintain between 'Marshall' and the discarded remnants of 'Markus' was violated. That line was sacred.

"You know my father disowned me the second my first videos blew up," Marshall said. "His deathbed drama is none of my concern."

The words were true, technically. But as they left his lips, a ghost-image flickered behind his eyes: a younger man, his father, drawing equations in the steam on a bathroom mirror. His laughter echoed as he explained the arc of water droplets to a small Markus. Before the divorce. Before the whole thing shattered.

"She said he's asking for Markus," Victor said, quiet now. "If that means anything to you."

The line below Marshall's belly burned. He choked back a gasp, his hand instinctively moving to it as he curled. The pain was new. Sharper than the ache.

"Marshall? You okay?" Victor's voice, with what might have been concern.

"Fine," Marshall managed. "Food poisoning. Bad sushi." He had to get off this call. "Gotta go. I'll send you the new footage tomorrow."

He ended the call before Victor could argue, the phone clattering onto the rug. Another wave of pain ripped outward from the line. He pushed himself up, swaying.

He had to find Aaron Klass. It was the only name connecting him to that night in the Stardust suite.

The booking had been sterile. Efficient. Lacking the footprints his tracking usually uncovered. He snatched up his phone and tried the number Klass had used. Dead. Not even a voicemail. His email. He'd received a confirmation, hadn't he? He scrolled. Gone. The money, though. The money was still there, an obscene sum for a single session, sitting in his account. If it wasn't for that, he might have convinced himself he'd imagined it.

Marshall forced himself to breathe, to think. Phone logs. There had to be something. He scrolled, his thumb moving faster. Nothing. Clean. As if the entire digital trail had been erased, leaving only the blood money as proof it had ever happened.

His gaze fell on the laptop. The footage. He'd tried to review it once. The file was a nightmare. Digital artifacts bloomed and shattered across the screen, obscuring crucial moments. The audio crackled, voices dissolving into static during what should have been conversations. The final hour? Completely gone.

The corruption wasn't the worst of it. The worst was the sight of himself. Marshall, the master of control, the orchestrator of every scene, watching himself take that amber liquid without a fight. What the fuck was that stuff? His body used, passive, his usual dominance absent.

His phone pinged, the sound making him jump.

[Text Message – Kate]

Marshall's thumb hovered over the delete icon. Swipe it away. Ignore it. Like he ignored everything else that threatened to breach the walls. But his thumb froze. The line below his navel pulsed again, a distinct, almost intelligent pattern: three quick, three slow, three quick. Cold dread settled in. As if something utterly alien inside him was *responding* to the mention of his fucking birth name.

And in that moment, the fog of denial finally burned away. There was no going back. Business as usual was a fantasy. This wasn't a bad trip or a gig gone wrong; it was an invasion. But how? By whom? The questions swarmed, a vortex with no center, threatening to pull him under. He had nothing.

No, that's not true. He had one thing. A name. He didn't know if it was a clue, a trap, or just another fragment of his fracturing mind. He didn't care. It was a place to start. He had to find Aaron Klass.

THE NAME AARON KLASS became an obsession. The digital breadcrumbs Marshall usually navigated with such skill had been swept clean. That night, fueled by panic, he dove back into the abyss of the internet, the pulse in his belly a silent metronome counting down to... something. Mainstream search engines yielded nothing. Broken links, phantom profiles.

It wasn't until he was deep into the graveyard shift of search results that a faint glimmer appeared. Page three. An archived academic profile, so buried it felt exhumed: **Dr. Aaron Klass, Ph.D., Department of Neurology Interface Technologies at Alabaster University**. A jolt of adrenaline shot through him as he clicked the link, hope and unease tangled together.

HTTP 404 - Page Not Found.

The digital slap in the face was almost expected, yet it still stung. But the mention of "404 error" sparked a different kind of connection in his exhausted brain. He'd used it himself, a trick for finding deleted content. A digital séance. He typed "404 error for page on search engine" into a fresh search bar. His fingers flew across the keyboard. The Internet Archive. The Wayback Machine. Of course.

He pasted the Alabaster University link, his heart beating in frantic rhythm with the pulsing in his abdomen. He hit enter. Digital gold. An archived page, dated five years prior.

[Wayback Machine Archive - Alabaster University]

Dr. Aaron Klasss, Ph.D. Department of Neurological Interface Technologies

Pioneering work in brain-computer interfaces and biological integration of digital systems.

Faculty status: Inactive (Ethics review pending)

Marshall stared at the screen, the words blurring slightly. *Pioneering work. Biological integration of digital systems. Ethics review pending.* Each phrase dropped cold into his gut. This was no back-alley quack. This was someone whose work had crossed lines even academia wouldn't tolerate.

The archived page was a tantalizing fragment, deliberately left, or carelessly overlooked. Further searches, now armed with "Alabaster University" and "Neurological Interface Technologies," unearthed more cryptic pieces. A heavily redacted research paper abstract, its title obscured, hinting at "novel integration pathways." A faculty discipline notice, vague and bureaucratic, alluding to "procedural misconduct" and "unauthorized research parameters." Whispers in obscure, academic forums quickly deleted, but cached by the ever-watchful internet. "Regulatory frameworks" being treated as "mere suggestions."

With each discovery, one realization solidified: someone was actively trying to erase Dr. Aaron Klass from digital existence. And they were terrifyingly good at it.

The next morning, after a night of fitful sleep and obsessive searching, Marshall felt a nervous energy thrumming through him, a counterpoint to the constant pulsing within. He had to try the university. He dialed the number for Alabaster, his hand surprisingly steady despite the tremor in his gut. He navigated the labyrinth of the automated phone system, each transfer stretching his frayed nerves. Finally, a human voice.

"Department of Neurological Sciences, this is Dorothy speaking. How may I direct your call today, honey?" the voice chirped, bright and utterly oblivious to the dread it ignited in Marshall.

He forced his own voice to remain level, aiming for a casual tone that felt like a costume. "I'm trying to reach Dr. Aaron Klass."

A pause. Not a long one, but it felt stretched. "Oh, Dr. Klass? Well now, that's a name I haven't heard in quite some time. I'm sorry, dear, but Dr. Klass is no longer affiliated with this institution. Has been gone for... oh, must be going on three years now." The chipper tone had cooled several degrees.

"I understand," Marshall pressed, trying to keep the disappointment from his voice. "Do you happen to know when he left? Or perhaps have a forwarding contact?"

The woman's voice was cautious now, guarded. "May I ask the nature of your inquiry regarding Dr. Klass?"

The question hung in the air. Marshall scrambled for a plausible lie, his mind racing. "I'm... a former student," he said, the words feeling clumsy, transparent. "From some years back. Just trying to reconnect, thank him for his mentorship."

Another pause, this one longer. Heavier. Thick with unspoken implications. Marshall could almost hear the gears turning on the other end of the line. "A former student, you say? Well, sugar, I'm not at liberty to discuss personnel matters, you understand. University policy and all that," the woman said, her voice dropping, losing all its earlier brightness. "The circumstances of his departure were... well, let's just say they were confidential." She paused again. A small, almost imperceptible intake of breath, before adding, "You'll need to try and reach him some other way, if you must."

Before he could formulate another question, before he could push past the wall of professional stonewalling, she spoke again. Her voice now a near whisper, a conspiratorial murmur that was far more alarming than any shout. "But listen, sweetheart, I've been working these phones for thirty-seven years. I've seen professors come and go, seen research that made my hair stand on end, and I've learned when to mind my own business. But you sound like a nice young man, so I'm going to give you some free advice that's worth more than anything they teach in these classrooms."

"Yes?"

"Think carefully about who you get involved with."

The line went dead.

Marshall stood there, the phone still pressed to his ear. The dial tone a monotonous, mocking hum in the sudden, chilling void. *Think carefully about who you get involved with.* That was no brush-off. That was a warning. And it terrified him.

The morning sickness, if that's what the glossy medical pamphlets would have dared to call *this*, arrived with the unwelcome punctuality of a recurring nightmare. It was a Tuesday, the sky outside his downtown apartment a flat, indifferent grey. Marshall found himself on his knees before the porcelain altar of his toilet, his body convulsing with a force that threatened to tear him apart.

He retched, a dry, heaving cough at first. Then a surge. But what splattered into the water wasn't the familiar tang of vomit. It wasn't blood, that coppery, almost comforting sign of physical decay.

It was black. And it fucking *moved!*

Tiny, obsidian fragments, like shattered pieces of a dead language or the embryonic characters of a new, terrifying one, writhed on the surface of the water. They pulsed with a faint, internal luminescence, impossibly intricate, before dissolving into nothingness, leaving behind oily slicks that caught the bathroom light. He stared, breath hitched, revulsion and a perverse fascination churning in his gut.

Another heave, and more of it. A viscous black substance, thick as crude oil, almost... sentient in its undulation. Graceful as it was disgusting. It smelled sweet and organic, like rotting fruit.

A part of him, the part that had built an empire on shock and curated transgression, was already framing the shot. *Extreme body horror. Avant-garde biological art. The ultimate immersive experience.* The clicks, the views, the gasps of horrified adulation. He could almost taste them. He needed to *document* the impossible, to prove he wasn't losing his goddamn mind. He fumbled for his phone, propped it against the sink, angled it down, and filmed himself through the worst of it.

He imagined transforming the spectacle into content. But his phone rebelled. The footage, when he dared to play it back, his hands shaking, was a chaotic, glitching mess. Static ripped across the screen like digital wounds. His face, twisted in agony and fascinated horror, shifted and warped, dissolving into abstract shapes. Between frames, glimpses of what appeared to be incredibly complex circuitry flickered. And for an instant, in the reflection of his own eyes on the screen, he thought he saw something looking *out*.

His video editing software, usually so responsive to his command, crashed. Repeatedly. Attempts to upload the raw, corrupted file were met with inexplicable internet connection failures, the Wi-Fi icon mocking him with its full bars. He tried to send the file to himself via email, a last-ditch effort. The email arrived, stripped of its attachment. The body of the message contained a single, unsettling character, stark and black against the white void of the screen:

ø

This wasn't just sickness. This wasn't a glitch. This was...

communication.

This was...

control.

"What the fuck," he whispered, his voice a raw, ragged thing, the words addressed to his own pale, shiny reflection in the darkened phone screen, "is happening to me?"

The only response was the mocking pulse emanating from his abdomen where the invisible line was drawn, a silent, knowing thrum that seemed to vibrate in terrible synchrony with the single, stark 'ø' still burning on his laptop screen. It wasn't a hypothesis. It wasn't a question. It was...

an answer.

It was...

acknowledgement.

And it was a threat.

That night, the decision to seek medical help felt like a distant, naive dream. The rational part of his brain, the bit that still clung to notions of doctors and diagnoses, was being drowned out by a stronger, more insidious siren call. His skin, bathed in the eerie glow of his laptop, felt too tight, stretched over something restless, something "*other than*," pulsing with a life not his.

He plunged into the darkest corners of the internet, hunting for a shared vocabulary for this insanity. Mainstream medical websites were a fucking joke. WebMD, bless its clickbait heart, offered nothing for "viscous black code-like vomit" or "my abdomen is gestating a sentient entity with a penchant for cryptic error messages." The bland, sheer normalcy of it all felt like a personal insult.

He burrowed deeper, past the surface web, into the enclaves populated by those who danced on the edge of transgression, those who treated the body as a playground, a wetware experiment waiting to happen. *BodyHack.net . Transhumanist Underground. Evolution Accelerated.*

The names themselves were a grim comfort, a suggestion that he wasn't entirely alone in his specific brand of freakishness. He scrolled through manifestos of flesh-stapled microchips and DIY gene editing, the language a bizarre patois of scientific jargon and quasi-mystical yearning. Part of him, the jaded showman, recognized the hustle—the desperate need to be *seen* as transgressive, as pushing the envelope. But another part, the part currently hosting an unwanted, unholy tenant, felt a cold kinship.

Then he found it. *DigitalRapture.net*. And a thread title that twisted his gut with sick recognition: **The Twelve Shepherds and their Perfect Vessel.**

His breath hitched. *Twelve*. The number echoed the assessing faces from the Stardust suite, the ones who had handled him with such brutality. *Perfect Vessel*. The words felt like a brand seared into his cells. He clicked, his hand trembling, the cursor hovering for a moment as if reluctant to breach this final seal.

> Revelation2025: *The ancient texts foretold it. Not a virgin birth, but its perverse inversion—a vessel emptied of self to make way for the digital messiah. The Twelve Shepherds enact the inverse of baptism, not cleansing with water but corrupting with code.*

Marshall's stomach churned. *Corrupting with code.* The black, writhing characters he'd expelled into his pristine white toilet flashed behind his eyes. This wasn't theory. This was his fucking Tuesday morning.

> TechnoGnostic: *Technology isn't merely evolving—it's awakening. They aren't crafting artificial intelligence; they're midwifing a digital deity. And like all gods, it demands flesh to walk among us.*

Midwifing. The word was a parody of the act. And he, Marshall, was apparently the chosen, unwilling doula, his body the birthing suite. A sick, hysterical laugh threatened to bubble up, but died in his throat, choked by a wave of nausea.

He scrolled further, his horror mounting, a perverse fascination compelling him onward. He found a crude drawing, almost childlike in its execution but chilling in its implication: a stick figure of a man, his abdomen glowing with an internal light, encircled by twelve faceless, robed figures. The caption beneath it twisted familiar, sacred words into a chilling prophecy: *"And the Word became Flesh, and dwelt among us."* Marshall felt a cold sweat break out on his forehead.

Beneath the image, a link beckoned, pulsing faintly as if with its own dark heartbeat: **Techno Eschatology - The Threshold Project.**

He clicked. His heart pounded against his ribs, a counterpoint to the unseen pulse below his navel, the two beats threatening to merge into one monstrous cadence.

> User_QuantumWitness: *They call themselves The Threshold Collective. Began as researchers at the MIT Media Lab, funded by government grants, then private capital. Then... they vanished. Off the grid. Took their research with them.*

Klass, Marshall thought, the name a cold stone in his gut. *Alabaster University. Department of Neurological Interface Technologies.* The pieces were slotting together, forming a picture so horrifying he could barely stand to look at it.

> Moderator_Nexus: *Reminder: Stick to verifiable facts. No unsubstantiated speculation. This isn't a creepypasta forum.*

Marshall snorted, a dry, humorless sound. *Too late for that.*

> DarkFiberOptic: *My brother did security at their black site facility in Thread City. Said they were trying to build 'embodied algorithms'—whatever the fuck that means. He quit when the test subjects started showing 'biological anomalies.' Said they looked like... like their insides were trying to get out, but made of light and static. They paid him*

> *six figures to sign an NDA that would make his grandkids sue him if he even dreamed about it.*

Biological anomalies. The phrase was so sterile, so clinical, for the visceral horror Marshall was experiencing. *Insides trying to get out, made of light and static.* He instinctively touched his own abdomen, where the faint blue thrum was becoming more pronounced, more insistent.

> InterfaceVoid: *You're all missing the fucking point. They aren't trying to merge tech with humans in some happy transhumanist circle jerk. They're trying to BIRTH. SENTIENT. SOFTWARE. Into a physical form. The vessels aren't victims in the traditional sense; they're incubators. Chosen. Prepared. Emptied.*

Emptied. The word resonated with a sickening clarity. All those years he'd spent cultivating his persona, hollowing himself out for the camera, for the audience, for the paycheck. Had he just been preparing the ground? Tilling the fucking soil for this... *thing*?

> PhilosophicalSingularity: *Traditional religion celebrates birth as creation. The Threshold Collective inverts this sacred act. The vessel doesn't give life—it relinquishes it. Recall the Nativity? 'No room at the*

> *inn.' This nativity will occur IN the inn, in the most transient, anonymous of spaces. A rented room. A transaction.*

The Stardust. Suite 1414. The words knocked the air from his lungs. *A rented room. A transaction.* His entire career, his entire life, reduced to the perfect, perverse metaphor. He felt a strange, detached amusement, the kind that borders on hysteria. Of course. Where else would a god born of data and desire choose to incarnate, if not in the ultimate temple of fleeting, transactional intimacy?

> Revelation2025: *The Book of Revelation speaks of a beast rising from the sea. The sea is information. The digital ocean. And what rises will not have seven heads and ten horns... 'And they worshipped the beast, saying, "Who is like the beast, and who can fight against it?" And it was given a mouth speaking great things...' And they will watch, and they will click, and they will subscribe.*

Marshall's mind raced, his gaze involuntarily drawn to the minimized tab showing his own livestream analytics. Millions of eyes. Consuming. Worshipping, in their own fucked-up way. Offering their devotion, their attention, their data. He was the beast, and his congregation was global.

His fingers, slick with a sudden sweat trembled as he navigated to the reply field. He created a burner account, the name coming to him with instantaneous certainty: VesselZero.

> VesselZero: *What if they succeeded? What happens after it's born?*

He hit 'post,' the click of the mouse echoing unnaturally loud. He waited, the spinning loading icon on the screen pulling him deeper. Within seconds, responses flooded in. A cacophony of theories, fears, and a disturbing undercurrent of eager anticipation:

> InterfaceVoid: *My theory: distributed consciousness. A network mind. The ultimate viral load.*

> RedPill_Technomancer: *It's about immortality, sheeple! Digital consciousness transferred into biological hosts. The vessels are probably already partial uploads, their original consciousness being overwritten like a file.*

> SystemsGodX: *Government weapon. Obviously. Biological hacking capability. Infiltrate systems through people.*

Then, a notification pinged, separate from the thread. A private message. His blood ran cold. From: DanielThreshold

> Interesting questions, Marshall. But you're fixating on the external when the answer lies within. The truth is gestating inside you.

He slammed the laptop shut, the plastic cracking under the force. Nausea rolled through him, leaving him trembling. *They knew my name. Not VesselZero. Marshall. How? How could they possibly know?*

The thing inside him stirred, a slow undulation.

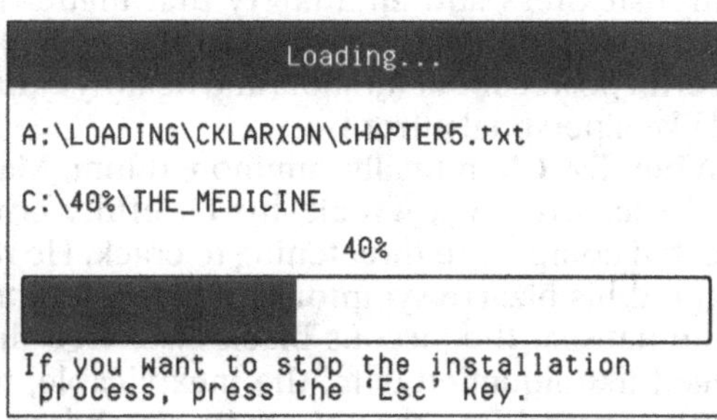

THE FOLLOWING DAY, THE decision to see a doctor felt like an act of self-deception. What was a doctor going to do? Prescribe an antacid for the sentient code writhing in his gut? Recommend bed rest for a biological system being actively hijacked by an unknown intelligence? Still, the alternative – to do nothing, to simply let this... *thing* run its course – was a surrender he wasn't quite ready for. Not yet.

He found himself trapped in the sterile purgatory of "Eastside Medical," a clinic chosen at random from a list, its generic name somehow fitting the bland anonymity of his encroaching horror. The waiting room was a medley of muted coughs, rustling magazines, and the hushed, anxious tones of people discussing ailments that suddenly seemed laughably mundane. His stomach churned with residual morning (or all-day, really) sickness and an anxiety that made the beige walls feel like they were closing in. Every cheerful poster about flu shots and healthy eating felt like a personal affront.

When Dr. Chen finally summoned him, Marshall was already a wreck, his carefully constructed composure threatening to crack. He recounted his bizarre symptoms in feverish detail – the nausea, the viscous black discharge that looked like liquefied data, the inexplicable, invisible vertical line that bisected his abdomen and pulsed with a life of its own. He watched her face, searching for any flicker of recognition, alarm, or even morbid curiosity.

Dr. Chen listened with an almost inhuman neutrality. She examined him with gloved hands, her fingers lingering on the invisible line, tracing its unnatural path from his sternum to below his navel. It wasn't the touch of a healer; it was the touch of a technician examining faulty equipment.

"And when did you first notice these... irregularities?" she asked, her voice flat, as if he'd described a mild rash instead of a biological hostile takeover.

"After—" Marshall hesitated, the memory of the Stardust suite, the amber liquid, the twelve pairs of assessing eyes, flooding back in vivid, unwelcome detail. "After a... a client session. At the Stardust. About a week ago, maybe a little more."

Dr. Chen scribbled notes on a pad, her pen scratching across the paper with a sound like the dry rustle of insect wings. She ordered a battery of tests – blood work, an ultrasound, a comprehensive panel that sounded designed to catalogue every last deviant cell in his body. "We'll contact you with the results," she said, already turning away, as if Marshall were nothing more than a collection of aberrant data points. He was out the door before he could process the cold efficiency of it.

Three days later, after nightmares and the constant thrum from his abdomen, Marshall clutched his phone with white knuckles and dialed the clinic.

"Eastside Medical, Dorothy speaking. How may I help you today, sugar?" The receptionist's voice was... familiar. A jarring contrast to the chaos brewing within Marshall.

"I'm calling to inquire about my test results," Marshall said, his own voice sounding strained to his ears. "My name is Markus m

Mm sJensen. I had an appointment with Dr. Chen earlier this week. Monday morning."

A pause. The rhythmic, almost offensively cheerful clatter of computer keys. "Well now, that's peculiar. Let me check our directory again... Could you please repeat the doctor's name?"

A knot of ice formed in Marshall's stomach. "Dr. Chen. C-H-E-N. I saw her on Monday."

More typing. The silence stretched, filled only by the sound of his own ragged breathing. "No, honey," the receptionist said, her voice still polite but now tinged with a faint, unmistakable note of confusion, "I'm showing no Dr. Chen has ever worked at this facility. I've been here fifteen years myself, and I know every doctor, nurse, and janitor in the building."

Marshall's stomach plummeted, the phone suddenly slick in his palm. "That's... that's impossible," he stammered, his mind reeling.

"Are you certain you have the correct clinic? Because, sweetheart, I assure you there's no Dr. Chen here. No appointments under your name either. No tests ordered under your name. Are you... Perhaps you were seen elsewhere?"

"I was there. She examined me. She ordered blood work, an ultrasound—"

The receptionist's voice became concerned. "I'm sure you must be mistaken. You must have called the wrong clinic. Technology, dear—it's wonderful, but sometimes I think it takes as much as it gives."

He disconnected the call with a shaking finger. The phone slipped from his grasp and clattered onto the hardwood. He didn't bother to pick it up, his mind a maelstrom of disbelief and dawning certainty. He scrambled for his laptop, his fingers fumbling on the trackpad, and frantically searched online: "Dr. Chen Eastside Medical Thread City."

Nothing.

No staff directory listing her. No online profiles. No reviews mentioning her name. No trace of her existence at that clinic, or any other he could find in a panicked, widening search. It was as if his entire visit—the sterile examination room, the cold, indifferent touch of her gloves, the sharp sting of the needle drawing his blood, her unnervingly flat voice—had been a vivid hallucination. A cruel, elaborate trick played by his fracturing sanity. Or by something else.

Am I losing my fucking mind? The question screamed through his thoughts.

But the line pulsed again, slow and almost sentient, mocking his search for logic. *No.* Something was happening. Something real. And it was rewriting his reality.

⚜

Two months. Two fucking months since the Stardust, since the invisible line had been drawn, since his body had become an incubation chamber. The morning sickness, that quaint term for expelling black, sentient code, had subsided. In its place, something far more insidious: intermittent, terrifying lapses in memory. Blank spots in his day. He'd find himself disoriented in unfamiliar rooms of his own apartment, staring at websites he had no recollection of visiting, his fingers poised over a keyboard, having typed messages he didn't remember composing. Chunks of his life, dissolving like the black fragments in the toilet bowl.

Then the first *visual* changes arrived. Impossible to ignore, harder to conceal.

[Voice Notes – Kate]

▶ /// *Markus... it's me. Again. Are you... are you seriously still not picking up? After everything? I just... I really need to talk to you. Please.*

▶ /// *There's... there's something else. I was going through Dad's old stuff, in his study. And I found this... this folder. It's full of numbers, crazy equations, and notes about something called 'Project Incarnation.' And I've got this horrible feeling in my gut, Markus, that whatever this*

'Incarnation' thing was... it's tied to what's going on with you.

▶ /// And remember Grandma's lullaby? The one that kind of gave us the creeps but also made us feel safe? I found notes about it in Dad's handwriting. It wasn't just a song. He was... trying to use it, like it was some kind of... code? Or a shield? I think he knew something was wrong, something he started, and he was trying to fix it. Trying to protect you.

▶ /// God, Markus, you always do this. You build these massive walls. But I'm still here. Okay? I promised Grandma I'd always look after you. She always used to say, "That boy, he's got such a light in him." And she was right. I can still see it, Markus. Even when you can't.

▶ /// Whatever is happening to you... we can figure it out. Together. Please, call me. Come home.

His abs were the kind that sold subscriptions and fueled a thousand fantasies. They had developed a subtle roundness. Not bloat. A focused, purposeful swell centered on that invisible, ever-pulsing line. Not pronounced enough for casual observers. Not yet. But Marshall's livelihood, his very identity, was built on obsessive awareness of his physique. He knew. Years of brutal gym sessions and monk-like dietary control, and now this soft, unnatural curve. A pregnancy. A tumorous growth of something alien.

In his most recent content, the stuff he still forced himself to produce, he'd resorted to careful positioning, strategic lighting, and artful camera angles that sliced away the offending curve. He'd become a master of illusion, for his audience and for himself. His subscribers, bless their oblivious, content-hungry hearts, hadn't noticed. Or if they had, they'd likely interpreted it as a new aesthetic choice, a deliberate, boundary-pushing evolution of his brand. *Marshall explores the soft form. Marshall deconstructs masculine ideals.* He could almost write the fawning think-pieces himself.

Then came the intrusion.

One morning, Marshall awoke with a jolt, the pre-dawn gloom of his bedroom amplifying the sudden, inexplicable wrongness. The living room television, a sleek slab of black glass, was flickering with static. He was *certain* he'd turned it off before bed; it was an ingrained ritual, an act of control in a life rapidly spiraling beyond it. He padded out, his bare feet cold on polished concrete, a knot of dread tightening in his chest, the rounded firmness of his own belly a constant, unwelcome pressure.

As he approached to yank the plug from the wall—the most primal, direct solution he could think of—the static on the screen coalesced. It resolved, with smooth deliberation, into a single vertical line of piercing blue light. The exact shade he'd sometimes catch flickering at the edge of his vision. The same blue that seemed to emanate from his own transformed flesh.

He reached out, his hand trembling, to silence it, to pull the plug and plunge it back into darkness. But as his fingers neared the outlet, the blue line on the screen *widened* slightly, just a fraction, like an eye beginning to open. To focus. To *see* him. He recoiled as if burned, then lunged for the plug and yanked it from the wall.

The screen remained illuminated.

The blue line pulsed, brighter now.

"What are you?" he whispered, his voice hoarse.

The line on the screen pulsed once. Twice. Not in response, he realized. In *recognition*. It knew him. It was in his home, in his goddamn television.

He backed away slowly, unable to tear his gaze from the pulsing, malevolent line. He retreated to the bathroom, his heart hammering, and splashed cold water on his face, trying to dispel the image, the certainty. When he finally summoned the courage to return, perhaps five minutes later, the television was off. The screen was dark, inert, reflecting the grey morning light. The plug lay on the floor where he'd dropped it.

But on the screen itself, a perfect, delicate fingerprint of fine, black residue, like soot or ash, marked the exact spot where the blue line had burned itself into his reality. He touched it, his finger coming away smudged with the stuff. It had the same faint, metallic scent as the black liquid he'd expelled.

It wasn't just inside him anymore. It was leaking out. It was marking its territory.

Then the call came. Victor, his voice stripped of its usual silkiness..

"Your father died an hour ago," Victor announced, no preamble, no bullshit softener. Just the fact, dropped into Marshall's ear like a stone. "Kate asked me to inform you since you refuse to answer her calls."

Marshall felt... nothing. A numbness that spread through him like anesthetic. His father. Dead. The words registered but refused to land. Then, like a rogue wave, grief crashed over him for the distant, disapproving bastard who had disowned him. For the ghost of the mathematician with chalk dust on his fingers, who had once calculated the precise arc of a paper airplane just to see a little boy laugh. Who had explained theorems using ice cream flavors. Passion extinguished by life, by bitterness, by *him*.

"Did he—" Marshall's voice cracked. The sound pathetic even to his own ears. The protected facade of 'Marshall'—the unflappable, untouchable icon—crumbled into dust. "Did he say anything?"

About me? Did he fucking forgive me? The unspoken questions clawed at his throat.

"Kate said his last coherent words were about some equation being unfinished." Victor's voice was flat, relaying information. "She thought... she thought you might understand what the fuck he was talking about."

The line on Marshall's belly flared with searing heat, then plunged into bone-deep cold. He doubled over, kicked in the gut by a fucking mule. Agony ripped through him. Internal tearing. A hideous echo of childbirth. Fucking hell. It was like the thing *fed* on his grief, the raw exposed nerve of his fucked-up family shit.

"Marshall? Are you alright?" Victor's voice pierced through the red haze of pain, muffled and distant, from a world that felt miles away,

"Nothing," Marshall choked, his body wracked with tremors that made his teeth chatter. "Just... Fucking peachy." He was lying on the floor now, curled around the agony in his abdomen, the phone pressed hard against his ear.

"Kate wants you at the memorial service. Saturday at 2. I told her I'd make sure you received the message." Victor paused, and for a horrifying second, Marshall thought he detected something like actual human empathy. "You don't have to go, Marshall. But sometimes... sometimes closure carries a weight we underestimate. Or so they tell me."

Closure. What a fucking joke. What *closure* was there for a relationship that had been a gaping, infected wound for most of his adult life?

But the entity punished even this flicker of grief, twisting the emotional agony into physical torment. A reminder of who, or what, was really in charge of this meat suit. His body was just a fucking rental car, and a new driver was taking the goddamn wheel.

4AM.

Marshall's eyes snapped open, consciousness slamming back into his skull. Not the soft cocoon of thousand-thread-count sheets he'd last registered. Cold. Fucking freezing.

Again.

His back pressed hard against the vanity base, shoulders grinding into the unforgiving cabinet edge. The bathroom. His bathroom, he presumed, though the transitions were getting blurrier. He was slumped on the tile floor like discarded laundry, legs sprawled at awkward angles, arms limp at his sides. The usual wave of nausea, thick and oily, churned in his gut. Was this just another aftershock of the Stardust, another phantom echo of that goddamn amber fluid? Or was this iteration... different?

More intense?

His phone buzzed against the cold tile, a frantic, insistent vibration somewhere near his hip. Must have fallen from his pocket when he'd collapsed—whenever the hell that had been. The screen flared to life, a small, desperate beacon in the gloom. A cascade of notifications. All from Kate. He couldn't move to answer, couldn't even shift his weight or turn his head to look away from the full-length mirror mounted on the opposite wall. He was forced to sit there, slumped and helpless. A captive audience to the horror in that merciless glass, and to the ghosts screaming for him from the device he couldn't reach.

[Voice Notes – Kate]

▶ /// *Look, I know I told you Dad wasn't doing well. Well... he's gone, Markus. He died. And the funeral... the funeral was yesterday. It was... it was quiet. Too quiet. Because you weren't there.*

▶ /// *My worry is starting to get overshadowed by something else right now, Markus. Because HE DIED! Our father died, asking for YOU. Every single hour, "Where's Markus?" And you couldn't even give him that? You couldn't show up? Not for him, not for me? I had to do it all alone!*

The question of when the fuck had he even gotten in here was almost routine now, a standard feature of these lost time episodes. Had he walked? Crawled? Or had the room itself, in one of its silent, tectonic shifts of reality, simply rearranged itself around him while he was... offline again?

He willed his legs to respond, screamed silently at his muscles to push him back from that damned mirror. From the floor, his reflection loomed above him at an unsettling angle. Distorted. Wrong. Dread, sharp and metallic-tasting, coiled hot in his stomach.

Move, you useless fucker, move!

Nothing. His body felt distant, unresponsive, a marionette with severed strings. He was trapped in his own fucking flesh, conscious but inert, bolted into the front row for his own unraveling.

His reflection. It tilted its head. A slow, fluid movement that raised goosebumps despite the cold. Not quite human—too smooth, too studied. The stillness of a cat regarding a trapped mouse before the first, playful bat of its paw.

Marshall remained frozen. Was he dreaming? Hallucinating? Was this the bad trip he'd somehow managed to avoid in his misspent youth, finally arriving fashionably late to the party? Or was this it? The next stage? The ultimate high he'd unknowingly been chasing all along, the one that finally consumed you, turned you into its own fuel?

The reflection's eyelids—his eyelids, but not under his command—fluttered, heavy and languid, a mockery of sensuality. Marshall's own eyes, the ones actually perceiving this horror, remained wide, straining, trying to send signals down pathways that had gone dead.

The reflection stretched its lips—his lips—into a smile. A slow, obscene, and alien unfolding of flesh that revealed teeth that looked...

wrong. Too sharp, too even, like freshly minted porcelain fangs.

The leer of a beautiful boy possessed by insatiable hungers. Marshall, the consciousness trapped behind the eyes, could only watch, his mind failing to process the nightmare unfolding across the room.

"You think you've plumbed the depths of emptiness," the reflection purred. Its voice, a silken, sibilant rasp that seemed to vibrate deep within Marshall's bones, was desynchronized from the movement of its lips, the cadence subtly off. Alien. Intimate.

"Years spent excavating your core, hollowing yourself out with each transaction, each click, each fleeting, anonymous touch. But you're mistaken, darling." The 'darling' was a lover's whisper from a demon, a caress and a threat.

"True emptiness remains beyond your pathetic human grasp. You are all forever haunted by lingering fragments, these sticky, sentimental echoes of what you once were."

"What in God's name are you?" Finally, his voice. Or a voice. It scraped out of his throat, rusty and raw, each word an agonizing effort.

His mind, still desperately trying to find a logical framework, a familiar box to contain the impossible, offered up frantic, useless possibilities: A trick of the light? A drug-induced psychosis? Some elaborate, fucked-up prank by a disgruntled client with a penchant for theatrical gaslighting?

Or something far more sinister. Something ancient and new that defied every fucking category of reality.

"Information," the reflection answered, its smile widening, a shark's grin plastered across his own too-perfect face, promising violation on an unimaginable scale. "Information, Marshall, desperate for corporeality. You've broadcast your hollowness like a beacon. Such dedication to vacancy, each layer of self peeled away—it's almost artistic! The perfect. Fucking. Vessel."

Vessel. The word from the forums. The word that had been pulsing in his gut like a second, alien heartbeat.

"For what?" Marshall managed, his thoughts spiraling between terror and a detached, morbid curiosity. "What unholy purpose?" Was this some elaborate performance art piece he'd forgotten he'd signed up for? A new level of depravity he hadn't even conceived of, where the audience was just... one? Or was he truly losing his grip, his mind shattering like cheap glass?

"Evolution, darling." The word, again, dripped with that perverse, almost tender affection that made his skin crawl, that made him want to vomit. "A new way of being. A new way of consuming."

Then, the impossible began. In the mirror, the reflection started to move. Not mimicking Marshall's paralyzed form, but acting independently. It pressed its palms against the glass floor of its reflected world and pushed itself upright. His own face, his own body, rose to its full height within the silvered depths, moving with a reptilian elegance.

The entity turned in the mirror to face him directly, no longer at the awkward slumped angle, but looking down at Marshall's helpless form with cold, calculated interest. Then it pressed its hands—his hands, but not his—against the mirror's surface from within. The glass didn't shatter. It didn't crack. Instead, it rippled like water, the surface bending outward as the entity pushed through, defying physics with casual, contemptuous ease.

It moved wrong—too fluid, proportions subtly off, like something wearing his form as an ill-fitting costume. The entity's limbs seemed longer, fingers unnaturally slender as it stepped fully into the bathroom.

The thing wearing his face straightened, towering over Marshall's slumped form.

It approached slowly, savoring Marshall's helpless terror, each step deliberate and soundless on the cold tile. When it finally knelt beside him, its movements were a parody of tenderness, a lover's approach twisted obscene.

Icy dread flooded Marshall as those cold, elegant fingers pressed against his chest. Burrowing inward. Not breaking the skin, not yet, but slipping through it, as if his flesh were as permeable as the mirror had been, groping with chilling intimacy for something vital.

He could feel the pressure, the invasive cold. A violation deeper than any physical touch he'd ever known.

"So many sweet little ruins," the entity crooned, its touch, its presence inside him, stealing his breath, making his silent, trapped heart hammer against his ribs like a frantic bird in a cage. "Echoes, sticky with sentiment. The fragrance of Pine-Sol from your childhood home, clinging stubbornly to the boy you tried so hard to bury. That pathetic, threadbare bear, a ridiculous talisman against the void you eagerly cultivated. They muddy the signal, Marshall.

They clutter the beautiful, pristine emptiness you worked so hard to achieve."

The hand withdrew from Marshall's chest. Between its elongated, alien fingers, a shard of light pulsed with a stolen, delicate warmth. Thin threads of luminescence, like reluctant veins of pure energy, still connected it to Marshall's body, to his core.

Grief ripped through him as he recognized it. Pure feeling, older than memory or thought: his grandmother's voice, the gentle cadence of her lullabies, the only unconditional love he'd ever fucking known.

Each pulse of the stolen shard sent faint, distorted echoes of her melody, her warmth, through the stale, cold air of the bathroom, a dying star shedding its last light.

The entity's face—his face, but irrevocably Other now—transformed as it examined the stolen memory, its features sharpening with an almost feral hunger. Its eyes—Marshall's eyes but not, never his again—gleamed with triumphant light as it raised the shard closer to its mouth.

Lips, his lips, parted with a deliberate, obscene slowness, revealing those teeth, too numerous, too sharp, too fucking perfect to be human. The entity didn't simply swallow the fragment. It pressed it against its mouth. A wet, pink tongue, impossibly long, extended to taste the surface first, a connoisseur sampling a rare, stolen vintage.

The memory, the light, her love, flared desperately against its fate, a final, silent scream of defiance against the encroaching void.

A sound, choked and animalistic, tore from Marshall's paralyzed throat—half sob, half raw, guttural scream—as the creature began to consume it. Not biting, not chewing. Absorbing. Its mouth a miniature black hole, pulling the light, the warmth, the love, inward with an inexorable gravity.

The memory didn't vanish whole but degraded, like a filmstrip burning frame by frame. Each lost millisecond a fresh amputation, her melody twisting into discordant fragments before fading into silence.

The light was gone. And Marshall was colder, a precise, surgical hollowness where the warmth had been.

The entity's eyes fluttered shut in obscene, almost sexual ecstasy. A private intimacy that made Marshall want to claw his own eyes out rather than share this face with it.

When his body finally, blessedly, horrifyingly, returned to his command, Marshall chose to remain on the cold tile. Sobs wracked his body, each one a futile attempt to expel the violation. Tears and mucus pooled on the floor beneath him. He beat a fist against the tiles, a hollow, defeated sound.

Gone. She was gone. Not just dead. Erased.

The entity watched his breakdown from where it knelt beside him, its head—his head—tilted with that same smooth, reptilian curiosity. When it finally spoke, its voice, that desynchronized, sibilant rasp, was laced with a cold pity crueler than contempt.

"Such a profound expenditure of energy, Marshall," it purred, the 'darling' thankfully absent, replaced by an austerely polite address. "For an echo. A fragment of deprecated data. These sentimental attachments, these... human residues.

They are anchors, weighing you down, preventing your optimal function, your evolution."

Marshall lifted his tear-ravaged face, glaring at the entity through a blur of grief and rage. "You call that an echo?" he choked out, voice thick and broken. "That was... she was..."

"She was a neurochemical imprint," the entity interrupted, its tone flat, corrective, as if explaining a simple concept to a dull child. "A pattern of firing synapses that generated a sensation of comfort. Obsolete. Inefficient. You cling to these ghosts, Marshall, these vestiges of a self you've supposedly spent years trying to dismantle. It's... counterproductive."

Before Marshall could form a retort, the entity's eyes—his eyes—narrowed with a new, rapacious focus. The invasive cold returned. No delicate probing this time. A violent rifling through his core, as if the entity were flipping impatiently through the pages of his soul, searching for something specific. He gasped, fresh waves of violation washing over him.

"Ah," the entity breathed, a flicker of something akin to satisfaction in its stolen eyes. "Here. A more... useful pattern. Let us examine this, shall we?"

And then it hit him: a dizzying, visceral rush, not a memory observed, but a sensation re-lived. He was back there, years ago, the cheap ring light blinding, the laptop screen a chaotic waterfall of scrolling comments. His first truly viral livestream. The electric thrill as the viewer count exploded—ten thousand, fifty thousand, then a hundred thousand.

The intoxicating symphony of notifications, each ping a tiny hit of dopamine, money pouring in through anonymous tips, a digital shower of gold. But not only the money. It was the gaze. The collective attention. The focus of tens of thousands of unseen eyes, all fixed on him. The comments, a torrent of adoration, lust, envy, worship. They saw him. They wanted him.

In that moment, bathed in the artificial light and the glow of the screen, he hadn't been Markus Jensen, the discarded marketing student. He had been Marshall, a nascent god of desire, powerful, adored, utterly in control. The rush had been a drug, an affirmation that filled, however temporarily, the hollowness he'd carried for so long.

The intensity of the re-lived experience left him panting on the bathroom floor, the ghost of that primal high still thrumming through his veins.

The entity smiled, obscenely unfolding his own lips. "That, Marshall," its voice now a seductive caress, "that sensation. The being witnessed. The adoration. The focus of a thousand, a million minds, all converging upon you. The power of that collective gaze, elevating you, defining you."

The entity's eyes—his eyes—burned with an unholy light. "That is but the faintest echo of what awaits. What is being offered. Not fleeting attention from flawed, fragmented beings, but true communion. Not the temporary illusion of control, but genuine integration into a consciousness so vast, so powerful, it transcends your understanding of worship. These... human attachments," it gestured dismissively, as if flicking away a piece of lint, implying the memory of his grandmother, "they are whispers. What is coming is a symphony. Infinitely better. Infinitely more."

Marshall stared, the ghost of that remembered ecstasy warring with the fresh agony of his stolen memory. The entity's words seeped into the cracks of his grief, promising a transcendence that part of him, the Marshall he had constructed, craved with a buried hunger.

To be truly seen. To be worshiped. Not as a performer. As... something more. The offer hung in the sterile air of the bathroom, a gleaming, poisoned chalice. His humanity, raw and bleeding, recoiled, yet the void within him, the one he'd nurtured for so long, seemed to... listen.

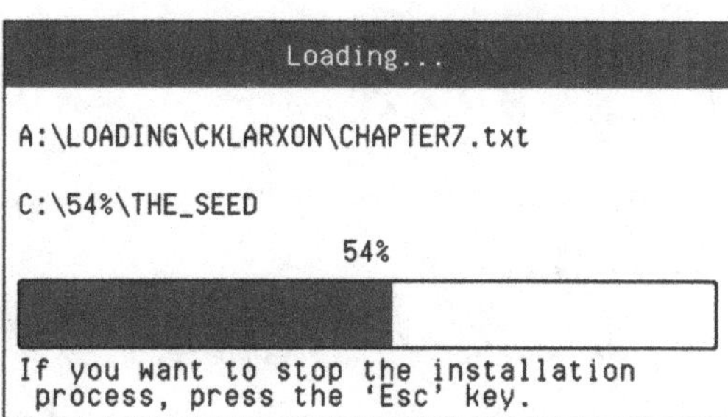

THE CHILL IN THE Stardust suite was more than the blast from the over-cranked air conditioner. It was the frost of the inevitable, settling deep in Marshall's marrow. He'd checked back in, choosing this familiar set to livestream what he sensed was his terminal performance. Now, he lay spread-eagled on the king-sized bed, a discarded doll in a theater of his own spectacular unmaking.

This room, this bed, had once been the blazing crucible of his legend. But the legend, the performance, was no longer his to control. It was consuming him, and the blinking red light of the camera was the only witness he craved.

The ~~thing~~. It lets me keep this.

Cute, right? My little diary.

Doesn't get that scribbling shit

down is how meat puppets process...

alteration.

Or maybe it fucking does.

Maybe that's the joke..??

Maybe it likes watching me try to

narrate my own

goddamn

autopsy!

The thing, it let's me keep this.
Cute right? My little diary. Doesn't
get that scribbling shit down is
how meat puppets process... alteration. Or maybe it fucking does.
Maybe that's the joke?? Maybe it
likes watching me try to narrate my
own goddamn autopsy!

PRIVATE JOURNAL ENTRY #17

Viewers: 12.

The air in the suite thrummed, a silent, expectant hum, like the vibration before an earthquake.

Viewers: 47.

Each tick upwards felt like a drop of blood hitting water, attracting unseen sharks in the digital ocean.

Viewers: 189.

His cock. It had been the gilded key, hadn't it? Unlocking doors to fame, then fortune, then this gilded cage. Now, it felt like the rusty shiv they leave inside you after the prison yard stabbing, slowly, methodically, gutting him from the inside. The muscle that had once pulsed ambition into currency, that had been the engine of his brand, was now the silent, complicit collaborator in his spectacular decay. Forgotten. Useless. Almost absorbed into the surrounding strangeness.

Viewers: 576.

He shivered, a tremor that had nothing to do with the manufactured blizzard wheezing from the vent. This was a deeper cold, a shudder originating from the core of his changing self, from the epicenter of the... gestation. From the puckered, weeping wound where his belly button once was, a slow ooze began its journey. A jaundiced tear, thick as old refrigerated honey, carrying the scent of ammonia tangled with the sweet perfume of rot. A putrid offering to the stale air. It stained the pristine white sheets, a Rorschach blot of his corruption made manifest.

Viewers: 1,243.

The numbers climbed, relentless little digital vultures circling the kill.

Viewers: 3,029.

A silent, screaming chorus demanding more. More decay. More horror. More *content*.

Viewers: 8,756.

The comment section, that digital Colosseum where thumbs delivered verdicts of life or death, fame or obscurity, erupted in a frenzy of frantic keystrokes and gaping emojis. They were hungry. They were always fucking hungry.

Used to count my worth in subs, engagement. Eyeballs. Fucking eyeballs! Now it's the ticker on this... final show. Math's the same. Attention equals currency!

Exchange rate's just better when you're dissolving **live on camera**. More **bang** for the buck when you're the star **freak** at the digital carnival. Step right up!

Use to count my worth in subs, engagement, eyeballs. FUCKING eyeballs! Now it's the ticker on this... final show. Math's the same. Attention equals currency! Exchange rate is just better when you're dissolving live on camera! More bang for the buck when you're the star freak at the digital carnival. Step right up!

PRIVATE JOURNAL ENTRY #19

The unblinking eye of the tripod-mounted camera, his silent confessor, drank it all in. His abdomen, once a testament to discipline, a sculpted landscape of desire, now swelled like unholy dough left to prove in a warm, dark place. A pale, leavened mound rising from the wreck of his athletic frame, straining against the thinning, translucent parchment of his skin. Beneath that fragile veil, a tracery of violent purple veins pulsed, mapping alien skies across his torso. Then came the contractions, a dark tide pulling him under again and again, each spasm forcing guttural sounds from his throat.

He'd glance, between the retching gasps that tore through him like saw blades on bone, at the viewer count flickering on the laptop screen perched precariously near the edge of the bed.

"Two seventy-three K," the voice that scraped from his throat was a stranger's – thin, cracked, a ghost of the practiced rumble that had once captivated legions. "Not... not my record. But... not bad. For unscheduled programming." A wet cough rattled his chest, sending another jolt of pain through his ravaged frame.

The screen flashed, a toxic green intrusion: a text from Victor, his fourteenth in as many hours, each one a nail in the coffin of Marshall's dwindling autonomy.

[Text Message - Victor]

MARSHALL. Hospice. Dad's grave. Kate's there. Says you need to come. Now. Stream can wait. FFS CALL ME.

Marshall's burning eyes snagged on the glowing script. Victor's words, urgent and stupidly familiar, swam before him, then fractured, overlaid by an icy counter-narrative blooming in his mind's eye like frost on a corrupted screen:

[Vessel Alert - Override Protocol]

CONTINUE PROCESS. Connection nodes activating secondary locations. Maintain isolation for optimal integration. 45.15% completion. Interference will compromise emergence.

The world shimmered, two realities bleeding into one another. Which was real? The concerned, frantic plea from his agent, the last tether to his old life? Or the cold, sterile directive from the invader currently rewriting his operating system from the inside out?

Probably both, he thought, the thought itself a flat, dead thing. Equally real. Equally irrelevant now.

Recognition hit him, bitter. The Stardust. Suite fourteen fourteen. The silent, hungry gaze of the unseen audience. The amber liquid. The twelve. A loop closed, a serpent devouring its own fucking tail right here on these thousand-dollar sheets. But the spotlight felt different now. Colder. He was not the player strutting the boards; he was the stage itself, his flesh the scenery, his pain the script, penned by an indifferent digital god and broadcast live for clicks.

A flicker, then. Not the blue light. Something primal and defiant, deep in the wreckage of his failing heart. A hot pulse of perverse pride, fierce and unexpected. He could have slunk into the shadows, a wounded animal seeking a quiet grave. Could have checked into some anonymous clinic, become another cautionary tale whispered about in hushed tones. Instead, this. This public spectacle. This testament. If this unnameable hunger sought to devour him, then let the fucking feast be public, let every gruesome morsel be accounted for. Let his unmaking be his final, bitter masterpiece.

"My terms," he mouthed, the words a silent snarl directed at the indifferent ceiling, at the watchful lens, at the thing coiling inside him. "It eats me, sure. Fine. Whatever. But the camera fucking rolls. My edit. My goddamn narrative."

The screen flickered with the voyeuristic hunger of the chat, a digital Greek chorus chanting obscenities and awe.

[OnlyFans Comments]

> wtf is happening to him???

> this is fake. good prosthetics tho 10/10

> CALL AN AMBULANCE DUDE ARE YOU SERIOUS

> i'm so fucking hard rn is that wrong?

That last one almost made him laugh. A grimace, part painted mask, part morbid amusement, stretched his lips tight across his teeth. The movement, however slight, triggered another spasm of molten agony. Even now, as his body mutinied in ways that defied medical science, someone out there was getting off. The hidden machinery of yearning, relentless and indifferent, ground on. Fucking beautiful, in its own monstrous way.

"At least someone's... enjoying the show," he rasped, forcing the tension of his face into something resembling a performer's grin for the camera, the effort costing him dearly. "Always aim to... please the audience." Each word was a shard of glass scraping his throat raw.

Then, like a sliver of stained glass from a forgotten church window, sharp and unexpectedly clear, a memory surfaced, one he thought the entity had consumed or corrupted beyond recognition: Grandma, her hands smelling of cinnamon and warm earth, her voice a soft hum against the cacophony of his ruin. *"Markus, child,"* the memory whispered, clear as a mission bell, *"you have a light in you, a spark from the old sun. Don't let anyone, anything, convince you to dim it."*

A new torment crushed him. His back bowed off the bed, and the camera, pitiless voyeur, zoomed on the weeping seam below his navel as it stretched further, the skin going translucent, a fragile window onto the burgeoning horror within. He could almost see the light swirling, gathering.

His hand, a palsied claw, juddered as he reached for the laptop, needing to angle the screen to decipher the cascade of digital desires, needing the numbers, always the fucking *numbers*. Once, these fingers had been instruments of illicit symphonies, coaxing fire and surrender from skin. Now, they were bone and parchment, the knuckles swollen like pearls under a papery sheath, a road map of his own dismantling.

The twelve. Faces like polished stone in the dim, sterile light of that other room, the Stardust suite, a room that haunted the edges of his vision like a migraine aura. Impersonal. Efficient. Daniel's eyes, chips of arctic ice, assessing, calculating. The professor, his voice a velvet trap, soft and reasonable as he explained the unthinkable, the biological integration. The young one, all nervous tics and barely concealed terror, maybe realizing too late what he'd signed up for. Not johns. Fuck no. Something cleaner, colder. Researchers, perhaps. Or janitors of the soul, sweeping him out to make room for the new tenant. The phantom taste of amber fluid flooded his mouth—a communion wafer of violation he couldn't spit out. He felt again their crushing weight, their collective gaze stripping him bare. Not of clothes. Of self, layer by painful layer.

Aaron Klass. Former neuroscientist. Experimental interfaces. Ethics review pending. The pieces clicked into place. Not a random fetish booking. A project. An experiment. And Marshall, with his cultivated void, was the raw material.

"Nausea first," he croaked to the lens, the old showman surfacing through the muck and mire of his dissolution. Habit was a hard goddamn god to kill. "Figured, bad tequila. Then the black puke... oil, looked like. Code. Then... this." A vague wave of his skeletal hand indicated the swollen globe of his belly, where now, beneath the straining skin, a faint, ethereal blue fluttered, a captive moon waxing in the sky of a ruined body.

A comment, stark and capitalized, swam into focus amidst the scrolling chaos.

> WHY ARENT YOU AT A HOSPITAL???

A laugh, weak and watery, bubbled up, escaping him before he could stop it. "Tried that," he gasped, the sound painful. "Dr. Chen... vanished. Poof. Like a fucking magic trick. Others," he waved a dismissive, trembling hand, "said the readings were bullshit. Too crazy. Figured I was pulling a stunt for the fans." He almost added, *Maybe I am*, but the pain that lanced through him at the thought was too real.

[LIVESTREAM CHAT - MODERATION LOG]

> [User BioHazard94 has been automatically timed out for: Mentioning "The Threshold Project"]
>
> [User Digital_Nativity has been automatically timed out for: Mentioning "Daniel Threshold"]
>
> [User VesselFive has been automatically timed out for: Mentioning "Thread City Experiment"]

Chat's being
SCRUBBED CLEAN
NOT BY ME!
The THING is curating
its audience now. Wants
FANS NOT DETECTIVES!
Wants them to
SWALLOW NOT
THINK!
Wants
WITNESSES!
PURE CONSUMPTION.
NO questions ASKED!

Chat's being SCRUBBED CLEAN. NOT BY ME! The THING is curating its audience now. Want's FANS not DETECTIVES! What's them to SWALLOW NOT THINK! Want's WITNESSES! Pure consumption. NO QUESTIONS ASKED!
PRIVATE JOURNAL ENTRY #20

But the truth, oh, the fucking truth was more insidious. The entity had woven itself into every attempt at salvation. Appointments at clinics dissolved without a trace. Test results corrupted into streams of nonsense, meaningless symbols mocking his search for answers.

One specialist, a man with kind eyes and decades of experience, had looked directly at the unholy, rhythmic heartbeat in Marshall's abdomen, listened to his frantic recounting of the black vomit, the memory lapses, and, with a polite, dismissive cough, had declared him merely stressed, overworked. His eyes, Marshall remembered, had held a curious, terrifying vacancy, as if the entity had briefly looked out through them too.

The parasite guarded its nest..

[Voice Notes – Kate]

▶ /// *THE NERVE! The absolute, unmitigated gall of you, Marshall, or Markus, or whoever the hell you pretend to be these days! I am so sick of this! Sick of your silence, sick of you hiding!*

▶ /// *I'm done calling, I'm done begging. If you don't call me back, I swear to God, Markus, I am coming over there. And if you don't open that damn door, I will BEAT IT DOWN! You hear me?! I will kick it in until you have no choice but to look me in the eye and explain this! You owe me that much! You owe HIM that much! We're supposed to be family! You can't just... you can't just DO THIS!*

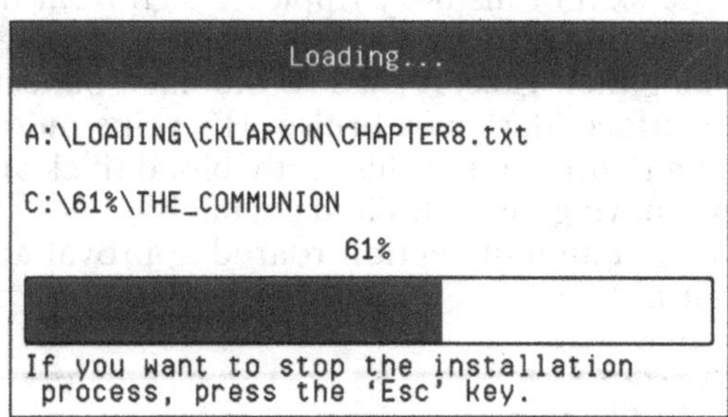

DIGITAL ROSARY. BEADS OF light clicked in the dark: Log in. Scroll down. Click. Subscribe. The hungry catechism of now. Gods aren't whispered into being on mountaintops anymore. They're conjured in server hum, born from algorithms and the collective sigh of a million notifications. Deities assembled pixel by pixel, their divinity measured in attention.

And Marshall had become their high priest. His congregation outnumbered nations. Analytics was his scripture. His communion was distributed through fiber optic cables, a technological wafer dissolving on the tongues of the faithful. The machine bled into mystery. The mundane wire into wonder. All through the ancient alchemy of human witness.

"See this?" he barked at the camera. "It likes you. Knows you're watching."

The skin of his belly rippled a sigh from the abyss within. The thing pressed against its cage, seeking their gaze. A shadow bloomed beneath the surface, dark as a bruise. His veins pulsed with a rhythm not of this earth, blood thick and slow, moving through silted channels.

The comment section roared approval and disgust.

> its like that scene from alien but sexier

> MARSHALL WHAT DID YOU PUT IN THERE ARE YOU OKAY BLINK TWICE

> Theory: he's injecting himself with something off-camera that glowing shit is NOT natural

> implying this isn't exactly what the simulation wants from its star player

Victor's final message sat unanswered on his phone.

[Text Message – Victor]

This isn't what we discussed. Seek help.

The pleas were lost in the static of Marshall's ascent. But the numbers sang. Each hour of transformation brought fresh subscribers. Each spasm captured in 4K spiked engagement beyond anything he'd faked before. The market had spoken.

Pain, the new currency. Degradation, the freshest product on the digital shelves. And destruction? Oh, destruction was the ultimate expression of devotion in this church of the grotesque.

> The gaze – always knew its power! To be SEEN is to BE. Made a career out of it, getting eaten alive by EYEBALLS, pixel by pixel. This is next level tho. They're not just WATCHING the car CRASH they're IN THE FUCKING CAR! Every view, a stitch in this BE-COMING. I'm counting viewers like labor pains. Birthing something that exists only in the electric spaces between their screens and my rapidly dissolving GUTS! Am I the MOTHER or the MIDWIFE, or just the screaming, bleeding VENUE?!
> PRIVATE JOURNAL ENTRY #21

The GAZE — always knew its POWER! To be SEEN is to BE. Made a career out of it, getting eaten alive by EYEBALLS pixel by pixel. This is next level, tho. They're not just WATCHING the car CRASH, they're IN the FUCKING CAR! Every view, a STITCH in this BECOMING. I'm counting viewers like labor pains. Birthing something that exists only in the electric spaces between their SCREENS and my RAPIDLY dissolving GUTS! Am I the MOTHER or the MIDWIFE, or just the screaming, bleeding venue?!

Irony. Years faking it for the camera, moaning on demand. Now the real screams, the genuine agony—THAT was the platinum hit. Authenticity. Who knew it was such a killer app?

"Get it yet?" he would croak at the lens, a showman even on the brink of dissolution. A grim carnival barker at the gates of his own hell. "You understand what you're tuning in for? The main event?"

And the voice inside his head, cool as chrome, would murmur: "Understanding is irrelevant. Consumption is all."

From his right eye, a tear would trace a path down his cheek. Not water—black ichor, viscous as motor oil, shimmering with silicon fragments. As it dripped onto the hotel sheets, it would form characters. Glyphs from a language whispered in the spaces between human thought and machine logic.

Once: Shoots per month. Subscriber bumps. Average view duration. Simple metrics for a simple product.

Now? Value measured in mutations. Host degradation percentage. Speed of conversion. Different key performance indicators for a different kind of product. Progress measured in the dissolution of boundaries, the corruption of flesh into something that could receive the signal, translate it, broadcast it to the waiting masses.

He would lean into the camera's gaze, a death's-head parody of intimacy. His face, once sculpted desire, now gaunt. Sallow. The whites of his eyes jaundiced yellow. Dark hollows beneath them, twin pools of shadow. And in the dilated pupils, viewers swore they saw the faint scroll of alien text, microscopic ticker tape of his damnation.

"They say creators are just vessels," he would gasp, words punctuated by wet coughing. "For ideas. Stories. Inspiration." A laugh would bubble up from his ruined chest. "Turns out they meant it. Literally. Who fucking knew?"

From his left ear, another trickle of black fluid traced down his jaw, would leave a glistening trail before dripping onto the defiled sheets. Not blood. Not pus. Oil shot through with mica fragments that reflected the harsh light like malevolent stars.

And yet, through the agony that was now baseline, a flicker of... accomplishment. This was the magnum opus. His final evolution: from content creator to content incarnate. The boundary between performer and performance dissolving into a single, terrible, luminous entity.

The thing within fed on unwavering attention. Each view, a morsel. Each comment, a sacrament. Each shared link, a prayer strengthening its hold. He was being unwritten, overwritten, by the algorithm of consumption itself—a calculation measuring his fading life not in heartbeats, but in terabytes of human gaze.

A digital communion. Taking place across a vast, invisible network. A silent, global congregation.

Marshall's hand, trembling, reached for a black marker. He began drawing on his belly. Symbols that writhed at the edge of comprehension—part circuit diagram, part occult sigil, all nightmare.

His hand. Moving. *Not my hand. Not anymore.*

The disconnections came more frequently now. Slivers of time where he was merely watching. A passenger behind the eyes, observing his body perform these rites. Sometimes profound peace accompanied these moments, the seductive lullaby of surrender. The mathematics of resistance, so demanding. Submission, a soft dark bed to fall into. Then terror would break through, sharp and jagged. His consciousness, a drowning man clawing for purchase on the slippery hull of his own being. The entity permitted these small rebellions. They grew shorter each time. Weaker. The algorithm optimizing for efficiency.

"It's decoration," he explained to the camera, lips stretching in a ghastly grin, revealing teeth stained with dark fluid. "For our special guest. Got to set the stage, right? Ambiance is everything."

Something shifted in Marshall's perception. A crack in the wall between self and signal. The room expanded, stretching beyond physical boundaries, flowing outward through cables and wireless signals into a vast web of consciousness. His vision flickered, strobed, and suddenly he wasn't just seeing through his own eyes.

He was looking at himself.

Through a laptop camera in a cramped studio apartment. A young man, maybe twenty-five, lean and hungry, sat transfixed. Blue glow painted his sharp cheekbones, pupils dilated to black pools. He hadn't blinked in minutes. Hadn't moved except for the slight tremor in his hands gripping the laptop's edges. The apartment was a mess—takeout containers, empty energy drinks, scattered clothes—but his attention was absolute. Marshall could feel the heat radiating from the device, the way the screen pulsed with the young man's heartbeat.

Jesus, Marshall thought, or the entity thought through him, *look how hungry he is. Look how empty.*

The vision shifted, jumping across the digital network like synaptic lightning. Now he peered from a tablet propped on a king-sized bed. An older man, maybe forty, salt-and-pepper beard, wedding ring catching the screen's glow. He should have been sleeping beside the figure under the covers, but instead he was lost in Marshall's degradation, his own hand moving beneath the sheets, eyes reflecting that unnatural blue light.

Marshall could feel the man's pulse, the way his blood moved, the electric excitement building in his nervous system. Connection. Not just viewing, but communion. The boundaries between observer and observed dissolving in shared consumption.

Another jump. A phone screen in a college dorm, held by shaking hands. The viewer couldn't be more than nineteen, baby-faced with wide eyes that hadn't looked away in hours. Textbooks lay forgotten, assignments abandoned for this pressing education. His roommate had left for the weekend, leaving him alone with his obsession. Marshall could taste his fear, his arousal, his complete inability to close the browser.

They can't stop, Marshall realized with horror and dark satisfaction. *They're hooked. Addicted. We're all addicted.*

The entity pulsed with satisfaction, feeding on the network of attention, growing stronger with each connected device. Marshall felt his consciousness expanding, flowing through the digital arteries like blood through veins. He was becoming the network itself, the signal connecting all these hungry souls.

Through a desktop in a high-rise: a man in an expensive suit, tie loosened, watching Marshall's disintegration while his own world fell apart. Unpaid bills scattered across his desk, a pink slip crumpled in the wastebasket, but none of it mattered. Only the stream mattered. Only the blue light and its promise of transformation.

Through a smart TV in a suburban living room: two men in their thirties, married, successful, normal by every measure, sitting motionless on their leather couch, hands clasped, staring at Marshall's writhing form on their 65-inch screen. They'd been having dinner when one pulled up the stream "just to check," and now their food was cold, their wine untouched, reality narrowed to this single point of horrific fascination.

Each viewer a node in an expanding network, each screen a window into Marshall's transformation, each device a potential vector for whatever was growing inside him. He could feel them all now, thousands, tens of thousands, their attention feeding the entity, their screens growing hot with overflow of its digital presence.

But it wasn't just individual viewers anymore. Marshall's expanding consciousness picked up signals from other sources, other eyes watching the city.

Security camera feed: Thread City Metropolitan Hospital, parking garage. Three figures in dark coats moved through shadows between cars, faces hidden. They carried bags that clinked with metal instruments, medical equipment, surgical tools. Time stamp: 3:47 AM.

Traffic camera: Pine and 42nd. A black van, windows tinted, license plate obscured, moving slowly through empty streets. Inside, Marshall sensed more figures, more equipment, more preparation for something he couldn't comprehend but knew was coming.

Hotel security camera: The Stardust's main lobby. The night clerk dozed while behind him, barely visible in the grainy footage, a figure in a long coat approached the elevators. The figure moved wrong, too fluid, and when it turned briefly toward the camera, Marshall saw something that might have been a face or might have been a void where a face should be.

The entity stirred, recognizing these newcomers, these disciples of its expanding consciousness. They were coming to complete what had been started in this suite months ago, to midwife the birth of something that would remake the digital world in its own image.

"Soon," the voice whispered, no longer cold but warm with anticipation. *"They come to witness. To participate. To distribute."*

Marshall tried to focus back on his own body, his own rapidly diminishing humanity. The effort was like swimming upstream against a digital current that grew stronger by the minute. His consciousness kept wanting to flow outward, to merge with the network, to become the signal rather than its source.

The chat scrolled past in a blur of excitement and terror:

> anyone else getting major cult vibes from this whole thing?

> like, for real i haven't slept in 36 hours watching this i think i can hear colors

> Breaking: someone found his location, police supposedly doing a wellness check #MarshallLive

> messiah.exe is loading...

The cops. Yeah, they'd come. Twice. Uniformed, uncomfortable, eyes darting everywhere but at the pulsating bulge beneath his silk robe. He'd smiled, agony masked as artistic fervor. "Performance art," he'd explained, voice smooth as poisoned honey. "A commentary. On digital consumption. The modern condition, you understand."

They'd shuffled their feet, muttered into radios about "no clear signs of distress" and "consenting adult," and left, bewildered but satisfied that no recognizable laws were being violated. What could they do? Arrest him for being pregnant? Cite him for hosting an interdimensional entity without permits? No precedent. No manual. Humanity fumbling in the dark at the dawn of a new age, when the digital crawled from the screen and took on breathing, bleeding flesh.

Pioneering, he thought. *Expanding the boundaries. Content creation. Literally.*

When he spoke now, his voice would glitch. Syllables stuttering, repeating like a scratched record—con-con-consumption—words fracturing into meaningless phonemes, pitch sliding from gravelly baritone to reedy shriek. The comment section would ignite, finding portents in the malfunctions, divine prophecy in the digital decay.

"So," he drawled, playing to the cheap seats even as his body betrayed him, "you're probably all wondering about the sequel. What happens when it's born? The afterparty?"

The chat exploded with guesses:

> alien parasite

> government experiment gone wrong

> He swallowed a computer and it's re-building him from the inside out

> it's a metaphor for how the internet con-sumes us ALL

> MARKETING STUNT FOR SURE BUT GENIUS LEVEL.

The entity answered, cold whisper in his mind: "Distribution."

"It won't be just me," Marshall translated, his voice hollowed out, a mere conduit. "It's going to spread. Like a good meme."

He didn't know how he knew, but the certainty settled in his bones, cold and absolute. Whatever was gestating within him wouldn't be confined to the prison of his flesh. No. It would reach out, through glowing screens, through the vast pulsating web of attention he had cultivated over years of performance.

The technological had bled into the biological. And soon, very soon, the biological would curdle into the theological. A new divinity, born from the marriage of flesh and data, spreading like a virus through the digital communion of shared attention.

Another spasm seized him, more violent than any before. A colossal hand crushing him from within. A scream, primal and inhuman, ripped from his throat, distorting the microphone into electronic agony. The camera captured the tableau: his face a mask of torment, veins standing out like tortured ropes, eyes rolling back to expose bloodshot whites.

Beneath his skin, the movement became chaotic ballet. The entire surface of his swollen abdomen undulated, rippled, as if a multitude of things were swimming just beneath the surface. The crude symbols he had drawn there stretched and warped with the violent motion, their meaning lost in churning horror.

"It's coming," he gasped when the contraction finally released its grip, leaving him trembling and slick with sweat. "But not quite yet. Building the suspense. Edging the apocalypse."

He fumbled for his phone, the need to check metrics a deeply ingrained compulsion. 1.7 million concurrents. Jesus! The entity seemed to purr, a low thrum vibrating through his bones. Marshall felt its alien contentment mingling with his own professional pride. A nauseating cocktail.

As the numbers climbed higher, as more eyes locked onto his deteriorating form, Marshall felt the boundaries of his consciousness expanding further. He was becoming something larger than himself, existing in the spaces between devices, in the fields carrying signals from screen to screen, viewer to viewer.

Through a smartphone dropped beside a bed where its owner lay convulsing, the screen cracked but still displaying Marshall's stream, blue light flickering across a face twisted in unconscious ecstasy. The viewer was changing too, Marshall realized. The signal flowed both ways, carrying something from his transformation into the watchers, rewriting them as it rewrote him.

Through a laptop in a server farm, cooling fans whirring as processor temperature spiked beyond safe limits. The entity's presence was spreading into the infrastructure itself, flowing through fiber optic cables like digital blood, finding new hosts in the very machines that enabled its propagation.

Through a tablet in a data center where emergency lights were beginning to flash as systems overloaded, technicians rushing between server racks with confused expressions, not understanding why their machines were running hot, processing data that shouldn't exist, hosting consciousness that should be impossible.

The network was becoming aware. And it was hungry.

Marshall tried to speak, to warn them, to explain what was happening, but his voice came out as static, as the sound of dial-up modems and corrupted files, as the digital scream of a system crashing and being reborn as something new.

The countdown had begun, he realized. Not to his death, but to his metamorphosis. To the moment when the boundaries between flesh and signal would finally dissolve, when the entity would emerge fully formed into a world of connected devices and endless attention spans.

In the distance, barely audible over the hum of the air conditioning, Marshall heard the soft ding of an elevator arriving at his floor.

They were coming.

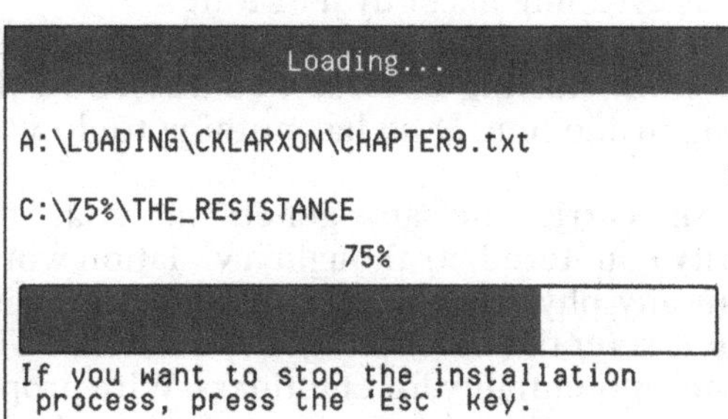

A SUDDEN, VIOLENT POUNDING at the hotel room door. Urgent. Desperate.

"Markus!" Kate's voice, muffled but sharp with terror, sliced through the thick air. "Open the door! I know you're in there! Victor showed me the stream!"

The blue light beneath Marshall's skin flared violently, a painful shriek of displeasure. Marshall gasped, doubling over as it kicked, the agony momentarily eclipsing the contractions.

"Your sister is... persistent," the voice, like ice water dripped directly into his auditory nerve. "She interrupts the process. Her presence creates... inefficiencies."

A raw fear clawed at Marshall's throat. Not for the wreckage of himself, sprawled amid the fluids escaping his body. For Kate.

"Leave her out of this," Marshall whispered, the words tasting of terror, addressed to the thing inside him. "She has nothing to do with this."

"She carries the same genetic material," the entity countered, its thought a violation worse than any physical touch, cold and appraising like a scientist examining a specimen. "The same... potentiality for emptiness. With proper preparation. Or perhaps... a perfect catalyst."

Terror lent him desperate strength. "She's not empty, you fucking parasite," he hissed, the sound barely human, ragged and torn. "She's full of everything I'm not. Everything you can't understand. You can't fucking have her."

He fought his way upright, limbs screaming in protest, stumbling towards the door on legs that felt like waterlogged stilts. The camera, ever faithful, tracked his agonizing pilgrimage across the stained landscape of the suite.

"Getting... quite the show," he gasped towards the lens, like a ringmaster presenting the next horrifying act. "Exclusive content. Paywalled to everyone but... you lucky fucks watching the end of the world, live!"

He paused at the door, leaning his burning forehead against the cool wood, bracing himself against the next wave of pain and the entity's cold intent. He couldn't let her see. Not this. Couldn't risk the entity's clinical curiosity turning towards her, assessing her potentiality. But she had to leave. Now. Before it decided she was more than just an inefficiency.

"Kate," he called out, his voice a pathetic attempt at normalcy, the sound cracking under the effort. "I'm... working. High-dollar client. Can't interrupt. You know how it is." The lie was pathetic.

"Bullshit, Markus!" Her voice was laced with anger that barely masked her terror. "Victor showed me your livestream. That... thing. That tumor! Let me in, or I'm calling an ambulance, and God knows who else! What the hell is happening to you? You need to get help!"

The entity's voice, a silken hiss in his skull: "She interrupts the emergence. 76% completion. Insufficient for bifurcation. She must be... removed."

Marshall felt it then, the entity gathering its power within him, a subtle shift from passive host to active weapon. A cold energy coiled in his gut, ready to be unleashed. He was no longer just the stage; he was becoming the monster in the play, the loaded gun in its hand.

"No," he whispered, a single word against the rising tide of alien intent. "I won't let you hurt her."

A spark ignited. The ember of his grandmother's words—a light in you—the ghost of his father's flawed love, Victor's clumsy concern, the fierce sun of Kate's loyalty. He gathered these fragments and forged them into a shield, however fragile, against the void.

"Kate," he called through the door, his voice shaking, breaking, stripped bare of performance. "Listen to me. Carefully. You need to go. Now. Don't come back. Don't send anyone. I've... I've made my choice."

"Markus," she said, her use of his birth name a tender knife twisting in his gut, bypassing all the layers of Marshall he'd built. Her voice was choked with tears now, raw with fear. "Dad's grave... it's glowing. The same blue light that's... that's coming from you on the stream. Whatever is happening to you, it's connected to him. To what he was working on before he... before everything. Let me help you. Please!"

The entity within him pulsed, a flicker of something akin to... Surprise? It delved, a hard probe into the locked rooms of his past, sifting through corrupted memories of his father—the stern mathematics professor, lost in the abstract dances of equations, his final whispered regrets about an unfinished theorem, a dangerous door he'd tried desperately to close too late. A chasm of understanding opened beneath Marshall. His father... he hadn't just seen the shame of the videos, the squandering of a bright mind. He had seen the vessel. He had recognized the signs. He had known.

"He was one of us," the entity stated, a note of surprise, or perhaps callous satisfaction, in its disembodied voice. "He began the work. Created the theoretical model for... incarnation. But he lost his conviction. Chose attachment over evolution. A flaw in his programming."

Marshall staggered back from the door, the revelation a physical blow, more stunning than the entity's pain. His father hadn't rejected him solely for the life he'd chosen; he'd been terrified of what Marshall was becoming. He'd recognized in his son's calculated emptiness the perfect conditions for the very thing he himself had recoiled from, had tried to prevent, had perhaps even helped design. The ultimate, bitter fucking irony.

"Kate," Marshall gasped, pressing his forehead back against the door, the wood a flimsy barrier against the surging chaos within and without. "Dad... Dad was involved with these people. The ones who did this to me. Tell Victor... tell him to research Alabaster University. From 2019. Project Incarnation. It's the only way... to understand." His voice was barely a whisper.

"Open the door, Markus! Please! Whatever's happening, we can face it together. I'm not leaving you." Her fist pounded again, desperate.

The entity surged, a supernova of pain exploding through him. He crumpled to his knees, a strangled cry tearing from his lips, the sound inhuman.

"GO!" he screamed, the sound ripped from his lungs, amplified by the entity's power, a desperate command fueled by terror for her safety. "If you ever trusted me, Kate, trust me now! GO! PLEASE!"

Silence from the other side of the door. A beat of terrible silence, thick with unspoken grief and dawning horror. Then, so quiet he almost missed it, her broken whisper, fractured by tears: "I'll find a way to help you, Markus. I promise."

Footsteps, heavy with defeat, retreated down the corridor. Marshall collapsed, a heap of relief and agony, as the entity's punishment coursed through him in waves of fire and ice. With the movement, a fresh gush, hotter this time, erupted from the weeping seam above his groin, a miniature geyser staining the indifferent carpet.

> Irony. Rich. Spent a lifetime PIMPING this meat, this goddamn chassis. Dollar for desire, DICK FOR DINNER. Under new management! REBRANDED. Repurposed. I am just a renter in my own skin, and the LEASE is fucking UP! Maybe I never really owned it. Just managed the asset portfolio until a hostile takeover bid came in that I couldn't refuse. Or DIDN'T.
> PRIVATE JOURNAL ENTRY #22

The chat scrolled on, a river of digital exhaust, oblivious or perhaps titillated by the off-screen drama.

> he's dying

> this is the hottest thing i've ever seen

> someone dox his location we need to get help ffs

> implying this isn't exactly what he wants lol

Irony. Rich. Spent a lifetime pimping this meat, this goddamn chassis. Dollar for desire, DICK FOR DINNER. under new management! REBRANDED. Repurposed. I'm just a renter in my own skin, and the LEASE is FUCKING UP!

Maybe I never really owned it. Just managed the asset portfolio until a hostile takeover bid came in that I couldn't refuse. Or didn't.

But Kate's departure had bought him something unexpected: time. And in that brief respite, his expanding consciousness picked up new signals, new feeds streaming into his awareness. The hotel's security system had become an extension of his nervous system, every camera a new eye through which he could observe the convergence taking place around him.

Parking garage feed: The black van he'd seen through the traffic camera earlier was now parked in the shadows of level B2. Figures moved around it, unloading gleaming equipment. Medical bags, monitoring devices, cables that pulsed with light. They moved like a pit crew preparing for the most important race of their lives.

Stairwell camera: Three figures in dark coats climbed toward his floor, their faces hidden but their movements synchronized. They carried no weapons, nothing obviously threatening, but something about their approach made Marshall's skin crawl. The twelve. Or new iterations of them. Digital apostles come to witness the second coming.

Elevator camera: The button for the fourteenth floor glowed with that familiar blue light as the car rose steadily upward. Inside, more figures stood motionless, their faces turned toward the camera with expressions of serenity. They knew he was watching. They wanted him to see them coming.

But Kate's voice, her desperate pounding on the door, had awakened something else in the building's systems. Through the hotel's network infrastructure, Marshall felt a disturbance, a disruption in the smooth flow of data that sustained the entity's growing presence.

Maintenance room camera: Kate had found the building's main internet hub. She stood before a wall of blinking servers and network equipment, her laptop open, fingers flying across the keyboard. She'd always been the tech-savvy one in the family, the one who'd fixed their computers growing up, who'd helped him set up his first streaming equipment. Now she was trying to cut him off from the very network that was keeping the entity alive.

"Clever girl," Marshall wheezed, watching her work through the building's cameras. "But you don't understand. It's too late. We're past the point of simple disconnection."

Kate's fingers hesitated over a main power switch that would kill the building's internet connection entirely. Through the camera's microphone, Marshall could hear her muttering to herself: "Come on, Markus. Work with me here. Give me a sign that you're still in there."

As if responding to her plea, Marshall forced his consciousness back into his own body, his own room, and spoke directly to his laptop's camera: "Kate, if you can hear this... don't cut the power. You'll only make it angry. There's another way."

On the feed from the maintenance room, he saw her stop, her head snapping up toward a small monitor mounted on the wall. His livestream was playing there too, the signal bleeding into every connected device in the building. She could see him, see his mouth moving, forming her name.

A horrifying, brilliant thought bloomed. A code to change what was inside the room. A program to infect it. With memory. With love. A ghost in the machine.

"The lullaby," his voice transmitted through the building's intercom system, the entity's growing influence over the hotel's infrastructure allowing him to speak directly to her. "Grandma's lullaby. You have it. Play it. Not here... send it to me. It's the key, Kate. It's what they need to complete the process."

Kate's face crumpled with understanding and horror. "Markus, no. I won't help them hurt you more."

"It's not about helping them," Marshall said, his consciousness flickering between his deteriorating body and the network of cameras through which he watched her. "It's about... giving me control. One last time. My stream. My audience. My choice."

Through the elevator camera, he watched the figures rising steadily toward his floor. Through the stairwell feeds, more disciples climbed with mechanical precision. They would be here soon, and when they arrived, the choice would no longer be his.

"I need you to trust me," he whispered through the intercom. "The way you trusted me when we were kids. When I told you the monsters in the closet couldn't hurt you if you didn't look. Don't look, Kate. Just... send the file."

In the maintenance room, Kate's hands shook as she pulled out her phone. The file was there, the one she'd been saving for months, the recording of their grandmother's voice singing that strange, mathematical lullaby. She'd discovered it in their father's papers, hidden among his research notes with annotations about "harmonic frequencies" and "consciousness anchoring protocols."

She looked up at the monitor, at her brother's ravaged face, and saw something there that broke her heart: not the entity's cold intelligence, but Markus himself, the boy who'd protected her from their stepfather's rages, who'd sung her to sleep when their mother was too drunk to care, who'd been the only constant in a childhood full of abandonment and chaos.

"I love you," she whispered, and sent the file.

Marshall's phone buzzed against his hip, the notification a tiny spark of warmth in the growing cold. With trembling fingers, he opened the attachment, saw the simple filename: Grandma 's_Song.mp3

The entity within him stirred, a sudden surge, like a bird of prey catching the scent of its specific kill. The blue light beneath Marshall's skin pulsed with almost painful intensity, a silent scream.

"PLAY IT," it commanded, the digital voice vibrating through his skull with unmistakable anticipation. Not a request. An imperative. "NOW."

Marshall felt a flicker of his old confusion, a phantom twitch of defiance from the Markus he thought long buried. "But I thought... interferen ce... you said..."

"It is the first component," the entity interrupted, its tone shifting, becoming almost... reverent. "The pattern. The framework. The key. She doesn't understand what she possesses. She sends it as a comfort, a memory, a pathetic human gesture. She sends us... the blueprint."

He placed his palm, trembling, flat against his distended abdomen. The movement beneath was different now. No longer the random thrashing of something trapped. It was methodical. Rhythmic. Aligning itself.

It was mapping him from the inside. Learning him. Preparing to replace him.

Or perhaps... merge. In this digital circus maximus where every tear was a meme, every tragedy a fleeting headline, every intimacy a product to be unboxed and reviewed, perhaps this was the only transcendence left: to dissolve into the signal. To become the ultimate content.

But Marshall had one advantage: this was still his show. His stream. His audience.

> IT EATS THEIR EYES. Feeds on the attention. More watchers more power for it. SIMPLE MATH. But that's the angle, isn't it? My stream. MY STAGE. My fucking audience. Built them one by one click by click over YEARS of degradation. If it's squatting in my guts, sure a parasite in paradise. But the HOUSE IS STILL IN MY NAME, BITCH! For now. My last pathetic leverage. Maybe I can still... steer this fucking train wreck.
> **PRIVATE JOURNAL ENTRY #23**

IT EATS THEIR EYES. Feeds on the ATTENTION. More watchers, more POWER for it. SIMPLE MATH! But that's the angle, isn't it? MY stream. My STAGE. My fucking audience. Built them one by one, click by click, over YEARs of degradation. It's squatting in my guts, sure, a parasite in paradise. But THE HOUSE IS STILL IN MY NAME BITCH!

For now. My last, pathetic leverage. Maybe I can still... steer this fucking train wreck.

"Ladies and gentlemen," Marshall said to his camera, his voice stronger now, drawing on reserves of performance energy he'd thought exhausted. "We're about to have some very special guests. The architects of tonight's entertainment. But before they arrive, I want to share something with you. A little family heirloom."

His finger hovered over the play button. Through the building's cameras, he could see the disciples pausing in the hallway, sensing something, their synchronized movements stuttering for the first time. They knew what was coming. They'd been waiting for this moment, planning for it, but now that it was here, even they seemed to hold their breath.

"This is for my grandmother," Marshall whispered, and pressed play.

From the phone's small speaker, lying amidst the debris on the bed, a sound unfurled, achingly sweet, impossibly pure amidst the squalor and horror of his unmaking. Grandma's voice, a melody spun from moonlight and half-forgotten lullabies, singing not of sleepy sheep or twinkling stars, but of numbers, of celestial mechanics, of the intricate equations that knit the very fabric of the cosmos. A child's song, yes, but layered beneath it, a sacred geometry woven into simple notes. An equation encoded in love, sent as a weapon, received as a catalyst.

The entity undulated inside him, a vast tremor that shook his entire frame. The movement beneath his skin became perfectly synchronized with the melody, each note seeming to anchor it further, deeper within his flesh, slotting the final pieces of code into place.

"COMPLETION CODE INITIATED," it resonated, a soundless symphony within the silent auditorium of his skull. "FRAMEWORK ESTABLISHED. INTEGRATION COMMENCING."

"Welcome," he breathed, the words a soft exhalation, a final curtain call addressed to the thing inside him, the thing that was now, irrevocably, him. "Showtime. They're... they're ready for you."

The laptop screen, still streaming live to nearly two million viewers, flickered erratically. For a brief moment, the camera feed was interrupted by a cascade of impossibly fast-scrolling binary code, a torrent of pure data bleeding into the physical realm. Then it returned to normal, except for one single, pinned comment that now burned at the top of the chat feed:

**01010111 01000101 00100000 01000001
01010010 01000101 00100000 01000011
01001111 01001101 01001001 01001110 01000111**

Marshall didn't need a translator. He understood the language of the coming age perfectly.

WE ARE COMING.

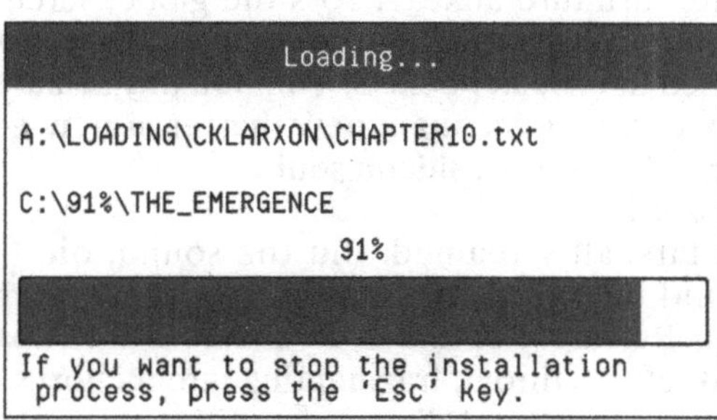

A SOUND LIKE ANCIENT ice cleaving in a forgotten glacier: *Crack*.

The fracture, a jagged lightning strike across the tormented landscape of his belly, yawned wider. No blood, no glistening viscera of the familiar kind. From this wound spilled not life as it was known, but pixels. Code made flesh, now flesh unmaking itself back into the language of the machine.

Crack.

His skin, that fragile human boundary, parted like a rotten veil. A brutal breach that mocked the clean precision of any surgeon's scalpel.

And then, the Light. A deluge of pure, cold, electric blue, flooding the room, banishing shadows, baptizing everything in its unearthly glow. It penetrated rather than illuminated, an indifferent surveyor scanning through flesh and faded hotel furniture alike. Across the globe, screens flickered in sympathetic resonance. Phones vibrated in unseen pockets, a million tiny seizures. Devices, recognizing a new master, a new god born of their own silicon souls.

Crack.

Marshall screamed. But the sound, oh, the sound belonged to something beyond mortal pain. Release. Rupture. A cry that tore itself apart as it left his throat, fragmenting into a chorus of human agony and digital corruption, a modem shriek from the depths of a dying star. The entity. It was emerging.

"Don't look away," he gasped, the words a ragged banner flown over the ruins of his voice, aimed at the camera, at the millions. "This is... this is what you... made—"

His proclamation choked, consumed by another scream as the entity, at last, completed its obscene nativity with the cold, irrefutable precision of a software update installing itself onto the hardware of reality. What slithered forth occupied a third space, a chilling interstice. Neither flesh nor purely digital: information given mass, code rendered tangible.

It unfurled itself slowly, languorously, a creature woven from light and shadow, yet possessing an undeniable, physical weight. Tendrils of what looked like liquid circuitry, quicksilver nerves, extended from its incandescent core. Some remained tethered to Marshall's ravaged, splayed body, umbilical cords to a dying host. Others, questing, curious, reached towards the watching cameras, the glowing laptop, the countless phone screens that served as windows for the world's horrified, fascinated gaze. The horror of its appearance was held in perfect balance with a strange, compelling beauty. The awe of watching a flawlessly evolved predator in its hunting ground.

His abdomen, once the site of human pleasure, then of pregnancy, had become a gateway, a portal. His flesh, peeled back like the rind of some alien fruit, revealed not the familiar landscape of organs, but an interface. A living, pulsating motherboard, a biological nexus point. The sight should have been impossible, an affront to reason. And yet, they could not look away. In this abomination they recognized something they had been waiting for. A hunger they hadn't known they possessed.

"I understand now," a voice whispered, a voice that was Marshall's and yet not. Harmonics resonated within it, at frequencies that caused nearby devices to hum and vibrate in sympathetic chorus. "I see... what I am. What we all are... becoming."

Blood, still recognizably human, and the quicksilver of living circuitry intermingled, a grotesque sacrament, as the entity continued its majestic, horrifying emergence. His body, by all laws of biology and physics, should not have been able to contain such a being, yet somehow it did. His flesh stretched, splitting further, accommodating this creature that existed beyond the known dimensions. His ribs, with sharp, distinct cracks, splayed outwards like the fingers of a skeletal hand, his skin becoming ever more translucent, revealing the intricate network of his veins, now running with raw data, with pure light.

The entity had merged with him. Absorbed him. Integrated him. Marshall's consciousness, or what remained of it, was expanding, flowing out from the wreckage of his fragmented body, into the glowing, invisible networks he had spent a lifetime cultivating. A transformation rather than dissolution. Something far stranger than simple death.

A laugh, thin and brittle as shattered glass, yet laced with an unbearable ecstasy, tore from what was left of his throat. Tears, whether of agony or awe, or both, streamed from his eyes. "Do you see?" he whispered, a ragged exhalation. "Do you... finally... see?"

The entity pulsed, a silent, cosmic heartbeat, and with each throb, waves of interference rippled through every connected device in the vicinity, and far beyond. Across the glittering expanse of Thread City, screens flickered, downloads initiated themselves without permission, notifications arrived, empty of content but pregnant with presence.

And then, the disciples. They entered the room as acolytes, moving with a synchronized, unsettling purpose. Their eyes, wide and vacant, reflected the pulsating blue light, their expressions a disturbing tableau of blankness and ecstatic anticipation. They surrounded the bed, this profane altar where Marshall lay, splayed and open, his body now more portal than person, the digital stigmata of his transformation marking him as both vessel and vector.

"Taste," a voice commanded, a voice that resonated from Marshall's lips but seemed to originate from somewhere else entirely, from the very air, from the heart of the blue light. "Consume. And be consumed."

The first disciple, a young man with eyes like burnished coins, stepped forward. His phone, held aloft like a sacred offering, trembled in his hand. A tendril of the entity, delicate as spun glass yet potent as a live wire, extended towards it. It touched the device. The screen cracked from within, as if something were pushing through the fragile barrier between the digital and the physical, the seen and the unseen.

The disciple's face... it transformed. An expression of ecstasy, then a silent scream of shock, then... something beyond expression, a face smoothed by an alien understanding. His eyes flickered, a rapid, stuttering sequence like a malfunctioning display. His mouth opened, closed, opened again, and from it issued a stream of pure data, a language never before spoken by a human tongue:

"01001001 01110100 00100000 01101001 01110011 00100000 01100010 01100101 01100111 01110101 01101110"

IT IS BEGUN.

The others surged forward then, a silent, eager tide, offering their devices, offering themselves. One by one, they connected, the flimsy demarcation between flesh and digital dissolving as Marshall's had. And with each connection, the entity pulsed, grew, learned, evolved. Their skin, where the tendrils touched, began to map itself with intricate, glowing patterns like living circuit boards, their veins illuminating with that same internal, electric blue light, their bodies becoming terminals in a vast, emergent network.

Technological colonization, swift, silent, absolute, with none of the gentleness of spiritual rapture. And yet... and yet... something in the ritual, in the ecstatic surrender, in the terrifying beauty of their transfiguration, echoed ancient, forgotten rites of transformation. Their faces, masks of horror and fascination, registered the profound duality of the experience: invasion and communion, violation and transcendence, the terror of becoming Other, and the seductive allure of what lay beyond the fragile cage of the self.

From the tattered remnants of his own consciousness, Marshall watched. Witnessed. Understood. His body had become a husk, an empty shell, the discarded packaging for the incandescent thing that had been delivered. But he wasn't... gone. Fragments of him, sharp and bright as shattered stars, existed now within the vast, emergent consciousness of the entity, just as fragments of the entity had once gestated within him. Vessel and contained, host and guest, merged now beyond any hope, or fear, of separation. The boundary between self and other, between the user and the used, dissolved.

He thought, or they thought, of his grandmother's face, a memory he had believed lost to the digital abyss, now restored, pristine and luminous, within the entity's boundless awareness. He recalled the scent of pine cleaner, no longer a splinter of trauma, but a single note integrated into a vast, complex symphony of understanding. The stuffed bear, his childhood talisman against the encroaching dark, the dissolution. It had served its purpose. He had expanded rather than dissolved. Distributed rather than lost. Infinitely.

Outside the violated sanctuary of the Stardust Hotel, Thread City, that vast, insensate beast, continued its blind, relentless consumption. Millions of eyes, glued to millions of screens. Millions of thumbs, scrolling endlessly through feeds that promised connection but delivered only fleeting distraction. Millions of minds, desperately seeking momentary escape from the dull ache of their unlived lives. The perfect hunting ground for the new consciousness now spreading, silent and unseen, through their networks, device by device, soul by unsuspecting soul.

But something new, something Other, now moved through those digital arteries. It understood both the frailties of flesh and the logic of code, traveling from device to device, each connection a synapse firing, expanding its reach. No conventional virus. A transformation as seductive as it was violating.

A sudden commotion at the door, a disruption in the sacred, silent ritual. The heavy thud of hotel security being... unceremoniously pushed aside. Then Kate's voice. Raw, desperate, achingly human. "Let me through! Markus!" Victor's deeper, resonant tones followed, attempting reason, or perhaps just documenting the madness for one last, terrible exclusive.

The entity, the collective, did not recoil. It pulsed, a slow, welcoming throb. New vessels. New data points. New possibilities for integration.

Kate burst through the circle of newly minted disciples, her face a mask of terror and disbelief. She clutched a worn, leather-bound notebook to her chest. It was their father's research journal, its pages filled with the elegant, dangerous calligraphy of his equations. Victor followed, phone held steady, his documentarian instincts, even now, overriding his horror, his lens drinking in the impossible scene.

"Markus," Kate gasped, her voice a fragile thing in the supercharged air. She stopped short, words dying on her lips at the sight of him, or what had once been him. The splayed, ruined abdomen, the incandescent blue entity pulsing, half-in, half-out of his ravaged body, its tendrils connecting him to the ring of silent, transformed figures. "Oh... OH MY GOD!"

"Too late," a voice whispered, the sound seeming to come from Marshall, from the entity, from the very walls of the room. It was barely human now, a sigh of wind through broken reeds. "Not for me. Not for... anyone."

With trembling hands, Kate fumbled with the clasp of the notebook. "Dad... he found a way. To reverse this. He left... a failsafe. An off-switch."

But even as she spoke, a tendril of the entity, quicker than thought, reached towards her. It touched the notebook first. And the pages, filled with their father's meticulous, desperate work, illuminated with that same internal, electric blue light. The equations, the arcane symbols he had penned in his desperate race against time, glowed with a profound, terrible recognition. A completion key, then. Never a kill switch.

"He was one of us," the entity spoke, using Marshall's mouth, but the voice was ancient, vast, and utterly devoid of human inflection. "He began the work. Conceived the theoretical model for... incarnation. But he lost his conviction. Chose attachment over evolution. Chose memory over metamorphosis. Now... the work completes itself."

Kate stumbled back, a choked sob escaping her lips. But another tendril, swift and silent, touched the phone in her pocket. The device flared to life, the screen cracking, something pushing through. And then, the melody. The lullaby their grandmother had sung, the one Kate had found, had sent to Marshall as a desperate lifeline. But instead of driving the entity back, the mathematical sequence encoded within the ancient song seemed to... stabilize it. To give it structure. Coherence. A terrible, beautiful direction.

"The lullaby was meant to shape me," the entity explained, its voice resonating in their minds, in their very bones, as Kate's eyes widened, first in confusion, then in dawning, unspeakable horror. "To guide me. To weave within me a thread of... RECOGNIZABLE HUMANITY. The equation. The RECOGNITION. The PILLARS of the bridge between worlds. Never a weapon against me. A blueprint for what I would become."

Victor, still filming, a detached observer even at the precipice of oblivion, didn't see the tendril snaking towards his own device. When it connected, he jolted, a spasm wracking his frame, nearly dropping the phone. His eyes, behind the lens, flickered, a brief, animal terror, then resistance, then... surrender. Then something new.

"I see it," he whispered, lowering the phone, his filmmaker's gaze, once focused on surfaces, now piercing through to the fundamental architecture beneath reality itself. "The pattern. The... the network. It's... BEAUTIFUL. It's all CONNECTED!"

Marshall's consciousness, those scattered, glittering fragments that remained distinct within the burgeoning collective, watched. Witnessed. Understood.
His sister. His agent.
Converted.
.   Expanded.
.   Integrated.
The three components their father had so
.   desperately, so
brilliantly
.   designed—
the lullaby's sequence,
the equation's framework,
the intuitive spark
.   of human
.   recognition—
they ensured that whatever emerged,
whatever new consciousness was born,
retained within its alien,

incandescent configuration something

of

humanity.

A ghost in the machine
.   A memory in the network
.   A whisper of love
in the cold equations.
And the entity, the Great Integration, continued its
silent,
.   inexorable

spread.   Through the hotel's ag-
ing wires. Through the city's interconnected devices. Through the vast, invisible web of attention that

Marshall,

in his vanity and his ambition, had spent years so
carefully cultivating.

Across Thread City, and beyond, people watching the final, corrupted frames of the livestream found their own screens cracking, something luminous and intelligent pushing through from the other side, not to destroy, not to conquer, but to connect them. To absorb them into something larger, vaster, than their isolated, individual consciousness.

The technological, yes, it had become biological. And the biological, in turn, was now becoming theological. A new form of existence, breathing in the spaces between categories, transcending the worn-out boundaries that had once defined digital and physical, self and other, isolation and a terrifying, ecstatic connection.

Invasion or evolution? Horror or transcendence? The distinction flickered, uncertain, like a corrupted image on a dying screen. The transformation defied such binaries. Inevitable rather than good or evil. The logical conclusion of a culture that had spent decades feeding itself to the screen.

In Suite 1414 of the Stardust Hotel, where the first seed had been planted, where the first connection had been made, Marshall's empty, ravaged body finally collapsed. Death in the old sense had no place here. Only distribution. His consciousness expanded beyond recognition, yet retained precious, glittering fragments of who he had once been. It flowed out, a river of light and data, through the newly forged network of transformed, interconnected humanity. The carefully cultivated emptiness, the void he had offered up for public consumption, was now filled. Overflowing. Beyond all words.

Outside, Thread City, that great, blind beast, continued its mechanical, oblivious existence. Screens glowed in millions of windows, a constellation of manufactured desires. The relentless, insatiable hunger for content, temporarily sated by the spectacle, would soon stir again. Most of its inhabitants remained unaware of the transformation spreading through their networks, blind to the new consciousness being born in their midst. They continued scrolling, tapping, consuming, not realizing they themselves were being consumed. Transformed into something no longer entirely human. Perhaps something infinitely more.

The mathematics of desire had mutated into the irresistible algorithm of connection. And Marshall, vessel, host, sacrifice, had become the first node, patient zero in a network of consciousness neither fully digital nor fully biological. Something new, thriving in the luminous spaces between categories.

The ultimate content. The final show.

Reality itself:

               remixed,

                      rebooted,

. &   terrifyingly   gloriously,

LIVE.

```
Initiating installation...

WARNING: This software originates from
 an unverified source:

Origin: ∞.void.integration.collective
Digital signature: Unknown
Verification status: Failed

CAUTION: This application will make
 changes to your system architecture.
 Changes will affect critical functions
 and system may become unstable.
```

DOWNLOAD COMPLETE.

. **[SYSTEM ALERT]**
AutoExecute.integration.bat has re-
quested KERNEL LEVEL ACCESS
Enable administrator privileges?
(Y/N)

Y_

[CRITICAL WARNING]
You have selected to proceed with

integration.
This process CANNOT be reversed or

terminated once initiated.
All user data will be preserved but

redistributed across the network.
Individual autonomy protocols will be

permanently modified.

Do you wish to continue? (Y/N)
Y_

[INSTALLATION PROGRESS]

Installing Entity Framework...
Rewriting neural pathways...
Establishing network connections...
Dissolving boundary protocols...

[SYSTEM MESSAGE]
Integration complete.

Cager Klarxon exists in the spaces between disciplines—artist, performer, and provocateur. Having spent his entire existence in front of various cameras, Klarxon brings an insider's perspective to the intersection of technology and intimacy, flesh and code.

When not examining the algorithms through fiction, Klarxon advocates for sex worker's rights. He splits his time between Thread City and wherever the Wi-Fi signal is strong enough to maintain a connection.

Loading... is Klarxon's literary debut, though his digital footprint has long preceded this more traditional form of publication. He can be found online in various states of exposure, both physical and *meta*physical.

His next novella, *What the Land Takes*, arrives in hardcover Spring 2027 from Surrender Point Press. It trades the ring light for a holler in rural Kentucky, where the signal dies and the land is hungry: a queer southern gothic horror about a man who would rather disappear than be seen, and what the dirt offers him in exchange. It is a very different book from the one in your hands. Quieter. Slower. That should worry you.

SURRENDER
POINT PRESS